Columbus On Fire

By
Quintessa Turner

Columbus On Fire © 2016 by Quintessa Turner

Printed in the United States of America

ISBN 13: 978-0-692-77413-7
ISBN 10: 0-692-77413-0

Cover Designer: AMB Branding Design
Editor/Typesetter: Carla M. Dean, U Can Mark My Word

Publisher's Address:
P.O. Box 18725
Erlanger, KY 41018

Social Media:
Facebook: https://www.facebook.com/author.quintessa/
Instagram: Author.qturer
Twitter: AuthorQuintessa
Goodreads: Quintessa Turner

Acknowledgements

First and foremost, I would like to give thanks to my Heavenly Father. Without him, there is no Author Quintessa Turner. Thank you Father God for all of the blessings, lessons, and every idea you have planted inside of me to help me be creative and unique.

My husband, Durrell Turner, thank you for being my backbone and number-one supporter throughout my career. Through the sun, rain, hell, and storms you kept pushing me until everything was done. My brother, Raekwon Behanan, thank you for all the late nights and early mornings, all the texting and emailing back and forth. Even though you were preparing yourself for college in New York, you still made sure I got this book done. My cousin, Author Jana Sullivan Behanan, thank you for all the encouragement, for pushing me on my word count, and rooting for me. My beautiful mother, thank you for just being you and supporting me. Uncle Reece, I can't thank you enough for supporting me. All the emails and phone calls paid off. Love is love, Unc! Last but not least, thanks to all my fans, family, and strong supporters. The wait is over. This is a true page-turner.

Columbus On Fire

Chapter 1

T
he music blared through the speakers as the DJ looped the chorus to B.M.F. (Blowin' Money Fast) by Rick Ross, hyping up the crowd.

"Yeah, y'all, I got the premiere!" DJ Self yelled as a mob of niggas took to the stage. "We got Brittany Hills in this muthafucka," he added, looping the chorus once again.

Poppa Joe and his crew were draped in so many diamonds, one would have thought it was a laser show the way the lights reflected off the stones. Stacks, the rapper of the crew, grabbed the microphone just as he and Poppa Joe were about to perform.

"I think I'm Big Meech, Larry Hoover," he shouted into the mic before telling the deejay to kill the music. "Hold it! Hold the fuck up!" he yelled, grabbing everyone's attention. "Fuck all dis bullshit. I been in these streets since I was a lil' cub, and being from Brittany Hills, it's one nigga I know been reppin' that blowin' money fast shit."

Stacks looked to his right at Poppa Joe, and then, as if everything had been orchestrated, the whole crew started rapping acapella style. The whole club went crazy.

"I told y'all I had that hot premiere," DJ Self yelled as he brought the music back in.

Poppa Joe stood shoulder to shoulder with his crew, smiling and rocking to the music while enjoying himself. With their chains swinging back and forth and while holding bottles of Ace of Spades high in the air, those Brittany Hills niggas let it be known they were about that paper. No sooner had Rick Ross' second verse started playing the crew from Brittany Hills began throwing money in the air while still on stage. The whole crew rapped as they grabbed the crotch of their pants and bounced around.

Things got so crazy inside Red Zone that the females turned the nightclub into a strip club, throwing caution to the wind as they got that freefalling money. The climax of the song moved many niggas to come out their pockets, feeling they had to be a part of the movement and join in with the rapping.

"These hoes terrible," Tamisha commented, turning her nose up as she watched females jump on the stage and scramble to get the money raining down on them.

"Bitch, please!" Layla responded, looking at her girl as if she were crazy. "You act like you ain't 'bout that life. Let a bill be due and your sponsor ain't playing fair. We'll see then how terrible a bitch gets."

Layla gave her girl Sasha a high-five as they turned to laugh at Tamisha.

"Fuck y'all," Tamisha quickly said, knowing her girls were right.

All three of them were at the club for different reasons. One for love, one for greed, and the other for a combination of things. Regardless, they were homegirls and you didn't see one without the other.

"Naw, bitch, fuck yo'self. You'll get better pussy," Layla responded, causing them to bust out laughing.

They were so caught up in their conversation that they didn't notice the waitress approaching their table.

"Compliments of Poppa Joe," the waitress said, setting several bottles of Ace of Spades down in front of the three ladies.

"Tell him I said thank you," Tamisha quickly replied as she reached to grab one of the bottles, assuming she was the reason they were sent over.

"Actually, they're for you," the waitress clarified, bursting Tamisha's bubble and surprising the hell out of Sasha.

Trying to hide her disappointment, Tamisha glanced at Sasha, who was looking across the room. When her and Poppa Joe made eye contact, Sasha smiled, mouthed the words "thank you", and blew him a kiss. Tamisha's eyes were stuck on Sasha, wishing she were her.

"Bitch, you better stop before you start something," Layla warned, trying to throw salt without it being seen.

"Oh shit, don't look! Here he comes," Tamisha yelled over the music. Her excitement returned when she thought of all eyes being on them once Poppa Joe made his way to them.

Poppa Joe and his right-hand man, Murder, maneuvered through the crowd, dodging conversations from those who were trying to steal a moment of his time. He continued moving steadily through the cluster of people until he reached the booth where the girls were seated.

"I hope I'm not invading ya'll space," he said, taking a seat next to Sasha.

"If you were, it wouldn't make a difference since you already made yourself comfortable," Tamisha replied, trying to make sure she was seen.

"You right," Poppa Joe responded, then leaned over to whisper in Sasha's ear. "I think you're beautiful, and I would love for you to bless me wit' yo' number."

While awaiting her reply, he grabbed one of the bottles and poured each lady a glass of the champagne.

Sensing her girls were envious of the attention she was receiving from one of the hottest niggas in the city, she quickly took his phone and programmed her number, adding it to his many other contacts.

"I'm not your average chick. It's more to me than meets the eye," Sasha assured him, taking one of the glasses from his hand.

"Only time will tell," Poppa Joe responded as he stood up, ready to make his exit since he already got what he came for. "I'll be calling you soon."

As he and Murder walked away, the music abruptly stopped.

"Get the fuck down!" Batman yelled, pushing a few niggas to the ground as he and his team raided the party. "Where's Poppa Ho...I mean, Poppa Joe's bitch ass?" he shouted while searching through the crowd for his man.

Poppa Joe was livid to say the least. If there was one person he hated more than anyone, it was Batman.

"This muthafucka thinks because he's the police, he can disrespect my name," he vented as he made his way through the mass of people.

"Here comes my bitch." Batman pulled out his gun when he saw Poppa Joe and his entourage coming his way.

The whole club grew silent. It was so quiet you could hear a mouse piss on cotton. There wasn't a soul in the club that wanted to miss this showdown. Fuck the song. This was truly a premiere, and everybody pulled out their phones to record the confrontation, hoping to be the first to post it on social media.

"Batman!" Poppa Joe yelled, stopping within arm's reach of Batman.

His crew quickly surrounded Batman and his whole team.

"The difference between a smart cracker and a dumb one is the smart cracker doesn't bite the hand that feeds them." Poppa Joe dug into one of his pockets and pulled out a wad of money.

"Watch your mouth!" Batman would not tolerate being

disrespected in front of his team.

"No, cracker, watch this," Poppa Joe told him, then threw a wad of money in his face. "Now go check the perimeter and make sure it's safe for me to leave."

Batman stood there with a look of disbelief about what had just transpired. As the onlookers pointed and laughed, Batman's anger grew.

"Muthafucka" he yelled, lunging at Poppa Joe.

However, before he could lay hands on him, the owner of Red Zone and his head security intervened.

"Get the fuck off of me! Get yo' fucking hands off of me!" After breaking free, Batman raised his gun and pointed it at the two bouncers. "Don't you ever put your muthafuckin' hands on me."

"Batman!" the owner yelled, seeing things were about to escalate. "You better look around and recognize what's at stake." He hoped Batman would come to his senses and just walk away.

Scanning his surrounding, Batman knew him and his team were in a fucked-up situation. The thought of going all out would be suicide. So, instead of doing the unthinkable, he fell back and allowed Poppa Joe to win this battle, but the war was far from over.

"Poppa Ho, we will dance again," he said, then turned toward his team as they made their exit.

"That's right, cracker. Leave before I turn you out and make you my bitch," Poppa Joe told him, showing out for the crowd.

Honestly, he was in his feelings that Batman would pull such a stunt.

"Play my song!" he yelled to the DJ, bringing the club back to life.

*****

After leaving the club, Poppa Joe pushed his all-black Porsche to the limit as he headed to his mansion in Savannah, Ohio. He couldn't wait to get there so he could express himself freely without incriminating himself in a club full of people who he knew were secretly praying for his downfall. The ride home seemed longer than the usual hour and thirty minutes.

"Fuck that cracker! I want him dead. I want his wife, kids, dog, and cat. I want everything living thing in his house dead," Poppa Joe yelled while pacing the floor of his massive living room. "I don't give a fuck what it's going to cost. I want him dead," he expressed, looking at his head henchman to carry out his order.

"Calm down, fam," Murder said, pouring himself a drink. "We definitely need to get rid of this problem, but we got to be smart about it. The whole city knows you and ole boy are at each other's necks, and if anything goes down, you'll be their number one suspect."

Murder took a sip of his drink, allowing Poppa Joe the opportunity to process what he just told him.

"Do it look like I give a fuck? I want that muthafuckin' cracker dead, and if his partner Big Country gets in the way, he can get it, too."

Not wanting to hear anything else other than his demands being carried out, Poppa Joe stormed out of the room.

Despite the fact that Poppa Joe stunted on Batman, he felt disrespected. Still, he held his temperament, not allowing his enemy the satisfaction of knowing he had gotten under his skin. It burned him up inside that the trailer park cracker felt like he was his equal, especially when he had judges, politicians, and law enforcement on his payroll.

"You chose the wrong muthafucka to dance with," Poppa Joe whispered to himself while standing on the balcony in his master bedroom. "I'll see you in hell."

*****

"Hold on a sec," Batman told his partner Big Country, then kissed his wife before heading out the door for work. "Like I was saying," he continued after placing the cell phone back up to his ear, "everywhere that motherfucker goes, I'm going to be there. I don't care if his ass jaywalks. I will be there to cite him a ticket. I don't give a fuck." He stopped to wipe the sweat from his forehead. "Damn, it's hot out here."

"Honey, come talk some sense into your daughter," his wife called out to him while rushing out the door. "She's talking about running off with that thug boyfriend of hers."

Batman turned and inhaled deeply. He couldn't care less what the little bitch wanted to do. One less mouth to feed, he reasoned.

"Let me go see about this girl," Batman told Big Country. "I'll meet up with you at the subway station."

After ending the call, Batman hit the remote starter for his car that was parked a few feet away. He wanted to give the A/C a chance to cool off the car's interior while he went back inside and acted like he gave a fuck about his daughter's situation. No sooner than he took a few steps toward his house, the car exploded, causing him to be thrown into the bushes.

"OH MY GOD!" His wife rushed toward her husband, not knowing if he was dead or alive.

Batman slowly emerged from the bushes. Realizing how close he had come to death, he gave thanks for his family crisis and wanting to cool off the car from the scorching heat. Otherwise, he would've been dead.

"Honey! Honey, are you okay?" his wife screamed, becoming hysterical as tears ran down her face.

"No time for questions. Get the kids," he ordered her.

Poppa Joe had gone too far. He was ready to kill his number one enemy.

*****

After relocating his family to Circleville, Ohio, which was thirty minutes outside of Columbus, Batman couldn't wait to push down on Poppa Joe's block. He was on his Denzel Washington shit from the movie *Training Day*, ready to take on the whole Brittany Hills.

He pulled up in front of Louie's, a hangout on that block, and jumped out of his wife's SUV, bulletproof protected and ready for whatever.

"What up, bitches?" he yelled, taking the crowd by surprise. "Y'all know who the fuck I am?"

Circling the front of his truck, he gripped his glock, wishing a nigga would try him.

"Y'all know who the fuck I am?" he yelled again, hoping to make an example out of a nigga. "I'm Batman," he continued once he felt he had everybody's attention. "And I'll have y'all asses in Lucasville doing twenty-three and becoming professional shit slingers. Now test me!"

Batman's head snapped around at the sound of one of the thugs laughing. He quickly walked down on him to see what he found so funny.

"You find me amusing? You think I'm funny?" he asked the man, but didn't give him an opportunity to respond. "You the type of pussy I would take to a gay boy and get them to fuck the shit out of your ass."

Batman stood so close to him that one would have thought they were about to kiss. Feeling uneasy, the guy backed up.

"Tell Poppa Ho I heard he gives good head and that I'm waiting for our next dance. If he knows what I know, it would look better if he came out of the closet before I expose his ass and allow him to be the little bitch that's screaming to come out."

Laughing a sinful laugh, Batman jumped back into the SUV and drove off. Although he had made Poppa Joe his number one suspect, Batman honestly didn't know who had tried to end his existence. It was a known fact that he had plenty of enemies, most of whom might take the opportunity to shoot a play his way when the spotlight wasn't directly pointed at them.

After leaving Brittany Hills, he made a few moves through the city putting motherfuckers on notice. He was definitely on one and Columbus was on fire.

Chapter 2

"Bitch, you crazy for giving Poppa Joe your number. He ain't nothing but bad news," Layla said while getting dressed. "You know Tone is gonna beat that ass if he finds out," she added.

"Girl, get you some business instead of worrying about mine," Sasha playfully responded, even though she was dead serious. "And fuck Tone's punk ass. He ain't running nothing but his mouth."

The fact that Sasha grabbed her cell phone to call Tone immediately after making that statement let her girls know who was really running things.

"Yeah, right," Tamisha said, knowing Sasha was faking.

Despite their on-again, off-again relationship, Tone was the love of Sasha's life. At times, she felt their relationship mimicked the lyrics to Mary J Blige's song, "Mr. Wrong". No matter what they faced, they got through it together. She loved her some Tone; he was her Mr. Wrong.

Unable to reach Tone by phone, Sasha became upset.

"Bitch, why the fuck you over there crying?" Layla asked.

Growing frustrated, Sasha slammed her phone down on the bed.

"Sasha! Stop it." Layla walked over to comfort her. "Stop thinking the worst. He's probably busy doing something and not able to answer right now."

"That's the problem! You never know dealing with him. He could be caught up doing something or he could be laying somewhere shot up and unable to..."

She couldn't make herself finish her sentence. Just the thought of him being hurt...or even worse dead...caused her to get even more upset.

"You can't keep taking yourself through this, Sasha. He ain't worth it. The sooner you realize that, the better off you'll be," Tamisha said, seeing it as a chance to add her two cents. "I'll be damned if I love a motherfucker more than I love myself. It just ain't in me."

Sasha shook her head at her girl. "That's because you've never had someone love you for you despite your flaws...someone who gave you a part of them that they haven't shared with another. Y'all know Tone, but I'm blessed to know Tony Jones," she said, letting Tamisha know there was a difference between the two.

*****

"Freddie, what the fuck you laughing at?" Tone yelled, returning five shots at the three niggas who were shooting wildly and trying to box them in.

"These bitches don't know who they fucking with," Freddie yelled back as he pulled out two twin short-nose 357's.

Freddie had named the two guns Czod and Jesus. Those were two names most people called upon in distress when asking for mercy and forgiveness, two things his guns didn't give.

"Freddie, they closing in on us!" Tone ducked down behind a car, putting his back against it.

Tone glanced over at his man and started sweating

18

profusely at the thought of them going down in a hail of bullets. Suddenly, Freddie, aka MJ, shouted out some orders to Tone, telling him to get at the one on his right while he took care of the two on his left. As if on cue, they emerged from behind the parked car that was riddled with bullets.

"They don't call me Michael Jackson for nothing!" Freddie yelled, then moonwalked through the flurry of bullets meant to kill him.

The bullet from the first shot Freddie let off hit the man square in the forehead.

"Yeah, bitch-ass nigga!" Freddie laughed and then quickly busted two more shots, this time aiming at the other dude and forcing him to take cover after seeing his partner go down.

Meanwhile, Tone had already handled his target with a shot to the chest.

Freddie quickly assessed the situation, and still in attack mode, he fired two more shots in the direction of where ole boy was hiding.

"Come out of hiding," he whispered to himself, patiently waiting with both guns ready to spark.

As soon as dude stuck his head out to return fire, Freddie shot him straight through both eyes like he was a marksman. The guy was dead before his body could hit the pavement.

"Come on, Freddie!" Tone yelled, hearing sirens approaching in the distance.

"Hold on. These muthafuckas probably got something in their pockets," he responded as he bent down to search them.

Despite all that was going on, Tone managed to take a second to glance at his phone and noticed he had a few missed calls from his girl. *Damn, she's gonna be tripping,* he thought. By the time Tone looked up, Freddie was running off between two houses.

"You real funny," Tone said after catching up to him.

"Whatever. Did you know those clowns?" Freddie asked while going through their wallets.

"Just some niggas from up north who I stuck up for a few pounds of loud."

"Well, smoke is on you when we reach the spot," Freddie told him, throwing the dead men's wallets in a trashcan before they jumped a fence to exit one yard and enter another.

"No doubt, fam. No doubt."

Both men laughed as they left the scene undetected and alive.

*****

"Poppa Joe, that cracker going crazy," Murder said, sipping on his drink. "He's running around this bitch pushing down on everybody's block."

"Fuck everybody else's block. Let that bitch push down on mine talking about suck his dick, and I'm gonna show him what type of dick sucka I am. No homo, my nigga."

Thinking of sucking, Poppa Joe picked up his phone to dial Sasha's number while imagining her sucking him off. When she didn't answer after a few rings, he disconnected the call. He wasn't the one to leave voice messages. He would train her to know that whenever she saw him calling, she was to drop everything and answer because his calls were definitely not ones anyone should miss.

"I'ma green light his ass and show him who runs this city and why muthafuckas love me more than the hate me," Poppa Joe said, feeling he was above the law.

Poppa Joe was to Ohio what Big Meech was to Atlanta. How Jeezy was linked to Meech, Gucci was to Poppa Joe. There were too many similarities to really distinguish between the two. Big Meech's billboard on I-75 said, "The World is Ours." Poppa Joe had his billboard on I-71, and it

20

read, "Why Wouldn't It Be?" That simple statement sparked many discussions and debates throughout the city, when each statement was actually one extension of another: *The World is Ours. Why Wouldn't it Be?"* Poppa Joe wanted Columbus to know.

*****

"Ooooh, bitch, right there," Batman moaned as the young chocolate thang rocked his mic like a true MC. "Yeah, baby, take that dick," he said, pumping her face at the speed of lighting. "Here it come. Ooooooh, baby, here it come."

Grabbing the back of her head, he filled her throat with his nut.

"Damn, baby, I needed that." He fell back against his pillow. "Girl, yo head so good I want to chop that shit off and take it home with me." He laughed while watching as her young, firm body slid out the bed.

"Yeah, right, your wife isn't having that." She laughed along with him while grabbing her blunt from out the ashtray.

Batman lay there not caring one way or another about what his wife was or wasn't having. Hell, she was lucky he didn't get on his *Harlem Night* shit and call home to tell the bitch he was never coming home. This wasn't Sunshine; it was Tasha B. But the way she had been sexing Batman's ass, she was just as addictive.

"You better be careful," she said as she sparked her blunt, snapping him out his thoughts. "Word has it Poppa Joe got it out for you."

"Fuck, Poppa Joe! He can suck my dick with lipstick on. I run this damn city."

The mere mention of his name made Batman uptight.

"I didn't mean to get you all upset. I was just letting you know what I heard, bae. If I didn't give a fuck, I would've kept the shit to myself," she responded, acting as if she was upset.

Tasha had a lot going on in her life. It wasn't that she was upset with the harshness of his tone, but rather, she didn't know if she should share the change of events in their relationship.

"Come here, girl."

Tasha took a hit of the blunt before placing it in the ashtray and sitting down next to him on the bed.

"I know you're concerned about my safety, especially after the incident with the car. I promise you, I'll be more careful. Now turn that frown into a smile," he said, showing her a softer side versus the things she had heard about him in the streets.

"Bae, despite our situation, I consider you to be my man. Even without marriage, I am your wife in spirit and in blood."

Rubbing her stomach, she let Batman know she was pregnant.

*****

"Special Agent Bailey, how are things coming along with the Poppa Joe case?" Special Agent Johnson asked his new partner while standing over her as she shuffled through some papers.

"No need to be so formal. You can just call me Angel," she told the guy who had just transferred from California. "And to answer your question, I'm using my creative mind and coming up with something that will have Poppa Joe and his crew eating out the palm of my hand."

Finishing her statement, she licked her lips slow and seductively, making her partner weak in the knees.

"You okay, Rocky?" she asked, laughing at the look on his face.

"I'm sorry, but my name isn't Rocky," he managed to respond.

"I know, but maybe his is," she responded and pointed at his erection.

Special Agent Johnson's face turned red from embarrassment.

"I'm sorry," he said and then quickly exited the room, leaving Angel laughing to herself.

Special Agent Bailey wasn't your typical agent. She was a hood type of female who grew up in the ghetto. She had seen firsthand the destruction drugs played within her community and how it destroyed families, even her own. She vowed at a very young age to be a part of the solution and not the problem in the war against drugs. It didn't matter to her all the criticism and backlash she received from family and friends. She had a job to do and wasted no time getting it done. Sure, no one she had ever arrested owned any poppy fields or had the resources to smuggle or transport drugs into the U.S. Still, she enjoyed the excitement of it all, the thrill of the chase and going undercover to catch the bad guy. She played her part so well that her suspects never saw it coming.

Chapter 3

"**G**irl, stop playing!" Tone playfully ran from room to room as Sasha tried to tickle him.

Days like this Sasha was truly at peace. She didn't have to worry about if Tone was safe since he was there with her and out of harm's way.

"You know I love you," she said after chasing him down in the living room.

"Come on, bae, that goes without saying. You my thug misses! How can you not love a nigga like me?"

While giving her a long hug, his phone began to ring. Sasha's whole demeanor changed when he reached to answer it. She knew the life she so badly wanted to protect him from was on the other end, calling him to partake in the forbidden ways of the world.

"Nigga, don't trip," he told the caller. "I'll be there within an hour. I got you!"

Ending his call, he saw the disappointed look on Sasha's face.

"Dig, bae, I got to make this move. I'll—"

"Don't even waste your breath," she said, cutting him off as tears fell from her eyes. "I worry about you so much; I'm driving myself crazy."

As Sasha stormed off towards the bedroom, Tone chased

after her. The last thing he wanted was to be the reason behind her tears.

"Bae, please don't do this. You know I can't stand to see you cry." He took her into his arms. "You know the life I live and—"

"That's just it." She pulled away from him and wiped her tears. "I know the life you live. I also know the danger of living such a life. When you leave out that door, there's a chance I may never see you again. There is a chance the life I dreamed of having with you will only be that, a dream!" she expressed while staring into his eyes, hoping he would understand and stay.

"What you want me to do, Sasha?" He looked at her, waiting for a response.

"It's not what I want; it's what *you* should want for *your* life, Tone."

Sasha continued lecturing him until it felt like she was talking to herself. Ultimately, she told him that it would be best if they were just friends because she couldn't stand to continue watching him waste his precious life doing dumb things.

Tone's nose flared up; he was not happy to say the least.

"All my friends chase cats, eat shit, and bark at the moon. So, miss me with all of that," he spat in anger.

After grabbing his belongings, he made his way towards the door. He stopped to take one last look at Sasha before slamming it behind him.

"She got me fucked up," he mumbled.

*****

"Big Country, talk to me, partner. What's the feel of the streets?" Batman asked his right-hand man as he drove from Tasha B's spot to go meet up with him.

"Shit sweeter than bear meat. I'm just waiting on you to pull up," Big Country responded, keeping everything under surveillance.

"Okay, I'll be there in ten."

Batman pushed his black SUV to the limit. It didn't take long for him to arrive at Lilley and Livingston where Big Country and several other undercover cops were waiting patiently for him at Will's Place.

"How many are in the house?" Batman quickly asked, checking his guns.

"Just him and two females," another vice officer replied as he snapped on his bulletproof vest.

"Okay, this is the plan. We in and out like a bank robbery. Secure the females and get them out of there. Leave Fat Daddy to me, and I promise y'all this will be a payday for all of us. Now who got the bogus search warrant?"

After seeing who had it, Batman looked at his five-man team and told them, "Let's ride."

It took no longer than a few minutes for them to load up and pull down Lilley with their battering ram.

"Columbus P.D.!" the officers yelled right before breaking through the front door.

Just like the trained professionals they were, it took them under a minute to secure the females and get them out of there, leaving Batman to deal with Fat Daddy himself.

"I ain't got shit to say! Take me downtown," Fat Daddy shouted once Batman entered the room.

"Calm down, big man, before I do more than grant you your wish," Batman threatened, taking the handcuffs off of him. "We already found the three keys of cocaine in this bitch. You know the time you facing? Calculate your bond, lawyer fees, and come up with a number to make me want to walk away."

Batman leaned against the countertop waiting on Fat

Daddy to reveal that magic number. Fat Daddy sat there wondering what kind of game Batman was playing. He'd heard stories before, but took them just as that.

"So dig, Batman, how I know if you for real or not?"

"You don't, but one thing I ain't gonna do is stand here and tongue wrestle with you about this shit. Either you get to shooting me some numbers or I'm taking your fat ass to jail. You choose!" Batman told him, ready to turn up on his ass.

"I got a hundred and fifty thousand." Fat Daddy said, throwing that figure out there and hoping it was enough to maintain his freedom.

"Make it two hundred thousand, and I'll have my guys bring the females back in so y'all can continue to do what it is y'all were doing," Batman responded.

"Fuck them bitches! You can keep them!"

Fat Daddy's response caused Batman to burst into laughter.

*****

"That was sweet!" one of the vice officers said, looking at the money spread out in front of him.

"Shit will only get sweeter as long as you keep your mouth shut and move when I say move," Batman told him while dividing up the money. "Big Country and I got a few more plays lined up throughout the city that will make this shit look like piggybank money. I'm eyeing Poppa Joe's operation, but being that he is good at what he does, it's gonna take longer than expected."

Part of Batman's plan was to tax the drug dealers who were selling drugs in his city. Those who didn't want to oblige would be eliminated. Fuck wasting good taxpayer's money sending them to jail. He felt the money could be better used somewhere else!

"You think they'll be good with getting seventy G's a piece?" Big Country asked Batman as they split seventy thousand dollars amongst themselves.

"Them four muthafuckas better be thankful to get that, especially with what I'm dealing with right now," Batman replied, his thoughts on Tasha B and his baby that she was carrying.

"I know you fuck with her heavy, but do you really think the baby is yours?" Big Country asked, not wanting his man to get too deep in the situation and the baby turn out not to be his.

"At first, I questioned the bitch. I was thinking she was on some hoodrat shit, trying to play me for some sucka. Then I noticed the change in the bitch from fuckin' with yo' boy to fuckin' with yo boy." Batman flexed like what else was there to say.

"What's the difference between the two or are they just one and then some?" Big Country asked, genuinely wanting to know.

Batman laughed, knowing his partner wasn't seasoned enough to understand hood terminology. Instead of keeping Big Country in the dark, he brought him to the light and gave him a better understanding.

"When we first started out, we didn't kick it or hang out. Now, we fuck with one another. We out here in the trenches making shit happen and wishing a muthafucka would get in our way. You feel me?" he explained.

"Oh, I understand now. She really fucks with *you*. You went from being her trick to being her man," Big Country stated, laughing like he had said something slick.

"You got jokes," Batman responded as he dialed the number for his pretty young thang. "While you being Mr. Comic View, she's the one who's gonna put us with Poppa Joe's stash houses"

Country's joking facial expression instantly changed to a serious one.

"Hey, bae," Batman said into the phone once Tasha B answered. "Be still. I'm on my way."

Without another word, Batman left his partner standing there with a confused look on his face.

Chapter 4

Sasha, Layla, and Tamisha were known throughout Columbus as the Spice Girls. Depending on your preference for women, you couldn't go wrong with whichever one you chose. Sasha favored Aaliyah to a "T". Even though Layla resembled Beyoncé, she couldn't find a man to put a ring on it for the life of her. Then there was Tamisha, the only chocolate candy out of the crew. She was the spitting image of Nikki Minaj but without the cash money behind her. Let her tell it, though, she was definitely in high demand.

"Bitch, pick your face up off the floor. We're hitting Paradise tonight," Layla told her girl.

"Yeah, you been on some lovesick shit, Sasha, and I'm tired of seeing you like this," Tamisha chimed in while searching through the closet to pick out an outfit for the both of them. "And, bitch, if you so much as mention Tone's name at any time tonight, I'm gonna punch you in yo' dick-sucking lips," she added, ready to turn up.

"I don't know, y'all. I ain't feeling it. I'd rather fall back and let y'all do y'all," Sasha said, pushing down on her girls.

"We going out tonight whether you want to or not. We going to talk shit, swallow spit, and watch these niggas try and fuck another nigga's bitch." Layla said and all three ladies busted out laughing.

"Since you put it like that, I don't see no harm in fucking with y'all tonight. Hell, I need a laugh or two fucking with this simple-minded nigga," Sasha responded while thinking about Tone, the one who she still considered the love of her life.

"Fuck that nigga!" Tamisha said. "We on our new shit."

Tamisha looked back and forth between her two girls to make sure they were all on the same page.

"If they knew better, they'll do better," they said in unison, wanting to put their own situations regarding their relationships, or lack thereof, behind them for the evening.

*****

No sooner than the girls arrived at the strip club and made it to the front door, all types of exotic whips started pulling up on the scene.

"Ahhh shit," Tamisha said, pointing at the cars. "It's going to be popping in this bitch," she commented, while handing the doorperson the admission for all of them.

"Why you say that?" Sasha asked, following her girls inside.

"Bitch, that was them Brittany Hills niggas pulling up, and if they in the building, you already know Poppa Joe will be, too," Layla said, answering for Tamisha.

Outside, nothing but all-black whips with the BHP logo on each side of the vehicle continued to pull up. Bentleys, Maseratis, Benzs, and every luxury car and SUV you could image lined up on Brice Road in front of Club Paradise. The strip club parking lot couldn't accommodate Poppa Joe's convoy. They weren't tripping. They just used one of the two lanes on the street to park their vehicles.

As if on cue, they exited their vehicles at the exact same

time, leaving the keys in the ignition. They were all on, wishing a motherfucker would. As they congregated on the sidewalk, the loud sound of a motorcycle could be heard approaching, as if announcing its driver's arrival. Heads turned in the direction they believe it was traveling.

"What the fuck!" Rab, KC and Shamar all said, pointing as the bike came down Brice Road.

It was a scene straight out of *Biker Boyz*, Sparks jumped off the pavement as the rider, who was wearing some slide-on steel-plated bottoms that fit under their shoes, rode top speed while standing on one side of the bike.

"That muthafucka on one!" Rab added, watching the rider finally jump on the seat of the bike.

Knowing all eye were on them, the rider popped a wheelie before setting it down, ending it with an endo. The whole crowd applauded as the rider slowly made their way through the parking lot near the entrance. Rab, KC and Shamar were the first to chase behind the rider, not believing what they had witnessed. It was one thing for a male to put his life on the line acting a fool on a bike, but it was something totally different and exotic to see a female put on like that.

"Damn, bitch! If you can handle that 1100 Yakaz like that, I know damn well you won't have no problems riding this 900," Shamar said, smiling while grabbing himself like he was working with those type of numbers.

The female smiled in response. Seeing Poppa Joe and his crew laughing at ole boy's comment, the female took it as her opportunity to make a statement.

"If your money is long and your tongue game is strong, you may just find out," she pulsed, giving ole boy false hope. "Being that you ain't nothing but the help, I'ma have to pass 'cause all I do is fuck bosses, and you ain't him," she finished while keeping her eyes on Poppa Joe as he entered the club.

Rab, KC, and the rest of the crew busted out laughing at Shamar's bruised ego.

"Come on, man," Murder said, putting his arm around Shamar's neck and pulling him close so he could whisper in his ear. "No sense in taking it the wrong way. Just use it as motivation to take your shit to the next level," he told him, then winked his eye at the mysterious lady as they entered the club.

Once everybody entered Club Paradise, the mood of the whole club changed. The male patrons who thought they were about to ball out quickly put their money away, downed the last of their drinks, and exited the club at the speed of forty horses when the crew from Brittany Hills showed up. The females who weren't turned up before were now turned up to the tenth power because they knew there was money to be made. Poppa Joe quickly bought out the bar and exchanged his larger bills for every single dollar bill in the building. He made it impossible for anyone outside his clique to patronize the dancers. He felt if there ever came a time when he couldn't do, his crew would be considered irrelevant, and that was something his crew would never be…not as long as he was around.

"These niggas got so much money they don't know what to do with it," Layla said, shaking her head as she watched them walk around throwing money in the air. "Had I known these fools was going to buy out the bar, I wouldn't have bought these damn bottles."

"Hell yeah, bitch! We could've saved that money for a rainy day," Tamisha said, adding her two cents.

"You right," Sasha said, interrupting her. "Excuse me," she called out, flagging down the barmaid. "Can you deliver these bottles to Poppa Joe and make sure to tell him they are compliments of the Spice Girls."

"Bitch! I know you done lost your mind sending our

bottles over to a nigga who already got a table full of bottles," Layla protested, as the barmaid walked off with the bottles in hand.

"Yeah, bitch! You tripping," Tamisha agreed, looking at the only bottle they had left.

Sasha laughed, but her girls didn't find any humor in what she had done.

"Y'all bitches complaining, and when I make a move to recoup our money, you silly bitches still want to complain. What the babies going to do?"

Falling back, the two women sat back and waited for her move to be put into play.

"Compliments of the Spice Girls," the barmaid said, setting the bottles in front of him.

"Who?" Poppa Joe yelled over the music, grabbing the young lady by the arm before she had a chance to walk off.

"Compliments of the Spice Girls," she repeated, then pointed in the direction of the three ladies.

Without any hesitation, he stood up and made his way over to them, taking the bottles they had sent over with him. When he moved, his entourage followed closely behind him like they were the Secret Service protecting the President.

"I like that in you," Poppa Joe stated as he sat down next to Sasha and placed the bottles on the table in front of them. "Had it been anybody else I would've felt some type of way."

He smiled as his crew took over her and her girls' section.

"I told you it's more to me than what you see in front of you. I might not have much, but what I do have, I don't mind sharing."

With those words, she let him know she wasn't just a taker but a giver, as well, and things would never be one-sided if he dealt with her. While staring at Sasha, he made a conscious decision to make shorty his.

The lights suddenly dimmed, grabbing everybody's

attention.

"Ladies and gentlemen, I have a special treat all the way from Atlanta. She goes by the name of Angel," the deejay announced and then added, "I just hope she's a naughty one."

As the lyrics to Mary J. Blige's "Mr. Wrong" started playing, Sasha became lost in thought about her Mr. Wrong.

"You alright?" Poppa Joe asked, noticing the change in her facial expression.

"I'm good," she quickly responded, realizing what could be accomplished if she were to get with a nigga like Poppa Joe. So, instead of worrying about Tone, she focused on the present and how rather than just dreaming of living a fairytale life it could actually become a reality.

Angel hit the stage wearing an all-white dance outfit with wings. She moved across the stage like she could fly, captivating her audience. Her eyes searched the crowd for one person in particular. Once they made eye contact, she seduced him from afar, while at the same time making every male in the place feel like they were the chosen one.

"Damn, that bitch is breathtaking," Shamar said, no longer mad that she had clowned him in front of his crew.

Losing the wings, she began doing a few tricks, turning things up. Her captivating performance moved the patrons to throw money at her from every direction. Some of the men couldn't contain themselves and tried to jump on stage, but the tight security succeeded in keeping them at bay. Angel loved the whole vibe of the place. She pointed directly at Murder, indicating she wanted him to come to the stage. While she waited for him to make his way to her, she worked the crowd for that last bit of money. She knew once she turned back around Murder would be there to collect the prize. Using her power of seduction, she mouthed the words to "Mr. Wrong" as she held eye contact with a few BHP niggas. She was setting them up for the grand finale.

"He be kissing and touching me," Angel sang, blowing a few of them kisses while she rubbed herself.

She stood straight up and extended one leg into the air, exposing her fat pussy through the material of her outfit. Suddenly, while holding that same position, she fell to the floor hard into a split, then slowly bounced up and down like she was riding a dick. The crowd went insane. Money rained down on Angel so heavily that you could barely see her on stage. She used that opportunity to undo her bottoms as the end of the song neared. Butt naked, she stood up slowly and gave the crowd a show to remember.

"Damn, that bitch's body is flawless," Rab commented as he watched her jump off the stage and into Murder's arms.

Rab, KC, and Shamar stood there envious because a bitch chose the next man. You would have thought with so much money being made between them, there wouldn't be any jealousy within their inner circle.

"That muthafucka is gonna get his," Rab told KC and Shamar.

Poppa Joe looked on in amazement as Angel freaked Murder. Slightly jealous because she didn't have his full attention, Sasha had to comment.

"The bitch will get down on all fours and bark like a dog if you paid her enough," Sasha told him as she poured herself another drink.

"What bitch won't? And please don't take that the wrong way. I'm just used to having my way and living the life I live. What one female won't do, the next will," he replied, giving her the raw reality of his life.

"I like you, though" he continued. "I really do like you, and I have more respect for you than to ask you to get down on all fours and bark like a dog. I want a chance to get to know you better and see where this could go."

Poppa Joe paused and waited for her response.

Sasha smiled at how he switched up from being arrogant. She nodded her head, letting him know that she was open to allowing the opportunity for them to get to know each other better.

"Now take this money and go buy yourself a few things before we leave tomorrow to go on tour with my man." As he stood to make his exit, he dropped ten G's in her lap. "And before you respond, no is not an option."

Then he disappeared into the crowd with his crew following right behind him.

"Bitch, you playing your hand like a muthafucka!" Layla shouted. "How much you hit him for?" she asked, wanting to cash in on her girl's play.

"I hit him for a little something, something. And you already know I'ma break bread with my girls. So, pause the game and let's see what your hand called for, because I know damn well you wasn't letting that nigga feel you all up and then walk away without getting yours," Sasha said, recognizing game.

"Girl, you already know! I had that nigga Stacks eating out of my hand. A bitch came up with a few dollars, but best believe he's gonna cash out if he wants to taste what's between these thighs." Layla high-fived her girl. "But until then, a bird in the hand is worth two in the bushes."

Layla extended her hand so Sasha could slap it.

"Matter of fact, where did Tamisha's trick ass disappear to?" Layla asked, looking around.

"Bitch, please. Tamisha is somewhere handling her business and not minding yours." Sasha laughed nervously and quickly changed the subject, not wanting to get caught up in what her girl was doing.

*****

"Oh shit, Tone! Right there! Don't stop. Please don't stop," the female yelled, loving the way he was pounding her. "I love it when you fuck me like this," she panted while throwing the pussy back at him.

Although Tone was there physically, he had zoned out mentally. He couldn't believe his girl had turned her back on him.

"How could you, Sasha? How could you?" he mumbled as he took his frustration out on the female lying underneath him.

Feeling his nuts tighten, he dug deeper.

"Here it comes! Ooh, here it comes."

Tone closed his eyes, anticipating his release inside her soaking wet pussy. The female, who felt his dick swelling inside her, waited for the exact moment were there was no point of return. Then, in one swift motion, she skillfully removed him from the warm confines of her pussy, slid down his body while still underneath him, and swallowed his dick into her awaiting mouth.

"What the fuck!" Tone yelled, as he nutted in her mouth. "Ooh shit, girl!"

After allowing her to drain the rest of his nut out of him, he fell back on the bed breathing heavily while trying to catch his breath.

"Bitch, you need to be arrested the way you just killed this dick," he said, smacking her across the lips with it.

"And I kill it every time," she shot back, sliding out the bed and preparing to leave.

"You ain't got to hit and run," Tone told her, sitting up. He wasn't nearly finished; that had only been the lead into what he intended to do to the pussy.

"Yeah, but being I didn't tell my girls that I was bouncing before I left, I don't need them killing my vibe by blowing my phone up wondering where I am," she explained while slipping her clothes on.

"Fuck them bitches!" Tone protested, hoping he could convince her to stay. "Tamisha, don't leave me like this," he added, hopping out of bed and showing off his erection.

She looked down at his stiff dick and then back up at him.

"Don't worry; I got you," she told him, removing her clothes once more.

For a moment, she wondered how Sasha would handle it if she ever found out about them.

To hell with that bitch, she thought, concerning herself only with putting her goals above everything else.

Tamisha was an opportunist who took advantage of any gainful situation that presented itself. She felt Sasha hadn't mastered the art of manipulation and didn't have what it took to exploit the people who were at her disposal. Even though Tamisha looked like Nicki Minaj, she was on her Lil' Kim shit remixing Yo Gotti's "Hood Anthem".

Chapter 5

"Tone! Tone!" Freddie yelled, coming out the trap spot. "Nigga, you won't believe who I just saw on the couch on *106 & Park*."

"Do I look like I give a fuck?" Tone responded, feeling some type of way because Sasha kept sending his calls to voicemail.

"Nigga, Czucci just premiered his new joint, "The Truth", on that muthafucka," Freddie told Tone, setting him up for what he really wanted to tell him. "That joint nice! Your bitch and Poppa Joe were sitting on the—"

"My what?" Tone yelled, cutting him off.

He knew about Poppa Joe pulling tight on his girl and that she was entertaining his conversation. What he didn't know was that Poppa Joe had put wings under Sasha's ass, flying her from city to city and exposing her to a life Tone could only dream of giving her.

"So that's why that bitch ain't answering my calls. Ooh, bitch, wait until I catch up with yo' ass."

As Tone stormed off, Freddie stood there laughing. Despite Tone being his man, he didn't care too much for Sasha. He felt she wasn't the type of female a nigga needed out there in the trenches. Tamisha, on the other hand, possessed everything a real nigga needed. She was willing to get her nails dirty while getting money with her man, whereas Sasha wouldn't.

"Nigga, you better pick the right one and forget about all that lovey-dovey shit," Freddie mumbled to himself as he turned to go back inside and put in that work with Tamisha.

*****

"Damn, girl, somebody's missing you like that," Poppa Joe commented, referring to the nonstop ringing of Sasha's phone. "I wish you would answer the motherfucker or cut it off because the shit is driving me crazy. Had I known the nigga was going to be feeling some type of way, I would've invited his ass along, too."

Everyone in the car laughed except Sasha. She couldn't believe Tone was blowing her phone up, and regardless of how badly she wanted to answer it, she couldn't. The only thing on her mind was gaining Poppa Joe's trust. She needed him to believe he was second to none, and answering her phone would not prove that.

"I got a better solution." Sasha pressed the button to lower her window. "Fuck this phone and whoever is calling," With that, she threw her iPhone out the window.

"Good choice," Poppa Joe replied.

His ego inflated even more at the fact he was able to make her quickly forget about her past situation and focus on the present.

"Now that that's not an issue, let me show you the life you were born to live," he told her, then kissed her hand softly. He knew it was just a matter of time before he had his way with her.

A whole month and eight cities later, Gucci didn't show any signs of slowing down. Poppa Joe had brought Sasha many clothes and shoes during the tour. Each city they landed in, he took her on a shopping spree so she could look her absolute best while on his arm. He had basically purchased her a new wardrobe, and whenever they arrived in a new city, they had to rent an extra SUV just to transport her things alone.

"You're doing too much," Stacks told him as they stood in the baggage claim area of O'Hare International Airport in Chicago. "You got us on some Mr. Bentley shit. It ain't like she got one or two pieces of luggage; she got enough shit to fill an SUV."

"Okay, Stacks, point taken," Poppa Joe responded with a chuckle.

Turning, he saw his new love interest heading their way. Within a short period of time, Sasha had elevated her position in Poppa Joe's world. He felt comfortable talking in her presence about things he wouldn't normally discuss outside of his inner circle. He was never one to talk business in front of any female he was laying pipe to.

"Hey, sexy," he said, greeting Sasha with a kiss on the lips as she stood there looking like a video vixen.

"Bae, would it be possible for me to shoot home and shoot back being we're only a few hours away from Columbus?" Sasha asked, hoping he wouldn't mind.

"Hell yeah, it's possible," Stacks answered for him. "And you can take all this shit with you," he added, pointing to several pieces of luggage she had accumulated over the course of a month.

Shaking his head, Poppa Joe laughed along with everyone else. "Since he put it like that, it might be best if you did take that trip."

Everyone applauded.

"Forget y'all," Sasha said, knowing she had hit Poppa Joe for a nice grip.

He had bought her any and everything she wanted, and

she couldn't wait to get home to show off everything to her girls.

*****

"Nigga, I'm tired of playing second fiddle to these fools," Rab said as he counted the take for that day.

Ever since that night at Club Paradise, Rab had been more verbal about his intentions. He was trying to convince Shamar and KC that it was their time to be kings of Columbus.

"We built this shit from our blood, sweat, and tears. We're the reason the streets respect B.H.P. We're the reason muthafuckas are checking that bread in."

He paused to see if they were feeling what he was saying.

"'Cause if not, niggas know our murder game is second to none," he continued with a bloodthirsty look in his eyes.

"Hell yeah, Rab," Shamar agreed. "Let's body these fake gangstas and run this shit, boss nigga."

"I'm with y'all," KC added, ready to take his place as one of the kings of Columbus.

Rab smiled inside. Everything he had dreamed of was finally going to become a reality. He knew in order for them to be successful in the execution of the takeover, their first move would have to be their best move, because if not, it could easily be their last. He had to be the mastermind and carefully plan out every move just like in the game of chess.

"That's what the fuck I'm talking about," Rab assured them. "I've been in communication with someone who will bring Batman on our side."

He had anticipated that bit of information would cause a disagreement.

"You what?" KC said, looking at Rab like he couldn't be serious.

"Dig, I know that shit might sound crazy, but you got to

44

trust me on this one. Ain't no sense in taking the top spot and inheriting Poppa Joe's beef with Batman. Not only that, but we need a few cops in pocket that we can manipulate and use to our advantage," Rab explained, painting the bigger picture and hoping they could see the forest past the trees.

"I'm feeling that," Shamar commented, having a better understanding of where Rab was coming from. "So when do we make our move?"

"In due time, playboy," Rab replied while rubbing his hands together. He loved it when a perfect plan came together.

*****

"I told y'all this shit was going to be easier than taking candy from a baby," Tamisha said, looking at the twenty pounds of loud they had just hit a nigga for.

"We should've kidnapped his bitch ass. I know he got a stash somewhere," Freddie said as he finished rolling a blunt.

"Yeah, but I needed to see if y'all could follow a bitch's instruction before we get off into some real-live gangsta shit," she replied, taking the blunt from Freddie.

"Bitch, who the fuck you think you talking to?" Tone yelled, not feeling the comment she made.

"Calm down, boo. It's not that serious," Tamisha told him.

She realized she was getting too loose with her lips. She knew she couldn't allow herself to get arrogant and expose her hand.

"Damn, can't a bitch feel like a boss amongst bosses?" she added, trying to lighten the mood and stroke a few egos as she passed the blunt to Tone.

"You can feel however you want as long as you keep putting together plays like this," Freddie said while pointing at the pounds of loud and thinking ahead to what would come next. "Fuck what that nigga talking about," Freddie added, referring to Tone. "He better recognize which side of toast is getting buttered, because that love shit ain't what it is."

Freddie wanted his man to face reality and wake up from that fairytale love story.

"Man, fuck that bitch," Tone responded, trying to fight between his pride and his heart.

His pride was telling him to forget Sasha and replace her with another. Then there was his heart, which wanted to see her and make things right.

"I hope that's what it is," Tamisha said, looking at him sideways. "When you start allowing your feelings to play out your pocket, it's time to change professions," she added before making her exit.

*****

"Damn, bitch, what the fuck?" Layla looked at the numerous pieces of luggage being carried into their apartment by a few BHP niggas.

"You can sit everything down over there," Sasha instructed, moving out of the way so they could retrieve the rest. "I can't stay long. I have to get back on the road," she told Layla as she headed to the refrigerator to grab something to drink.

Out the corner of her eye, she could see Layla simmering with envy. Her jealousy almost made Sasha laugh out loud.

"Has Tamisha made it back home or is she still missing in action?" Sasha asked, turning around with a bottle of water in her hand.

"Yeah, she showed up right after you left with Poppa Joe, and you won't believe the company she's been entertaining lately," Layla replied with a smirk.

46

There was no doubt in Layla's mind that Sasha would find the information entertaining.

"Who girl? What bum is she kicking it with now?" Sasha questioned, knowing her girl surely knew how to pick them.

"Wouldn't you like to know?" Tamisha said, surprising her two friends as she stood at the entrance of the front door.

*****

Oh fuck! one of the corner boys said to himself as Batman passed him while creeping down 4th Street.

Tone and a bunch of Short North niggas were shooting dice in the courts, while Freddie was on the far end capping at a female for some head. All of a sudden, they heard the sound of screeching tires.

"What the fuck?" Tone yelled.

As he scrambled to his feet from the kneeling position he had been in, his gun dropped from his waist. Determined not to get caught, Tone bent down to snatch up his gun. By the time he looked up to finally run, he saw that Batman and Big Country were damn near right up on him.

"Fuck!" While he cursed himself for not moving fast enough, the unthinkable happened. Shots were fired, forcing Batman and Big Country to take cover. Tone gave thanks for whoever let their gun bust.

"Get the fuck down!" Batman yelled as he turned back towards the dice game once the threat of gunfire ceased. "Y'all motherfuckers like playing with guns? Go chase my money the wind blew away," he ordered, picking the biggest one lying on the ground. "And the rest of you motherfuckers get on your knees and put your hands behind your head."

While Batman barked instructions, Big Country held everybody at gunpoint. Once the big fellow finished picking up what he could, Batman ordered him to do the same as the others. One by one, Batman ran through all their pockets, stuffing all the findings into his.

"I'm taking your money, phones, jewelry, and drugs, and I dare one of you bitches to say something," he challenged as he pushed each one back to the ground once he finished searching them.

"Y'all Short North motherfuckers think y'all tough?" Batman continued after finding a few guns during his search. "Then y'all got the nerve to take a shot at me and my boy like we one of these hood motherfuckers. Y'all got the game fucked up!" he shouted, pushing the last one to the ground.

Batman walked back and forth, kicking dirt in their faces and wishing one of them would jump bad.

"I'm the judge, the jury, and the prosecutor out this bitch. The sooner y'all realize it, the better off things will be." He looked around the courts as a small crowd began to gather. "I'm Batman and I run this muthafuckin' city!" he yelled for everyone to hear as he and Big Country returned to their SUV.

"We hit a nice lil' lick fucking with them niggas," Batman told his partner. "But did you get to see the one that got away?"

"No, because no one didn't get away," Big Country replied, thinking Batman was playing with him.

"Yeah, Country, one got away. I had my eye on him. He was bent down on his knees, and as he scrambled to his feet, he stopped to scoop up something off the ground. Then the shots went off and the motherfucker used that split second to get ghost. It's like whoever busted off those shots did it so that he would be able to get away," Batman reasoned, putting it all together.

"Damn, I missed that one," Big Country said in frustration, feeling he let his partner down.

"Don't worry, big fellow, I got his face sketched in my

mind. Best believe, we're gonna run into his ass again," Batman told him as his thoughts wondered to what he was going to do with the drugs they had confiscated. After all, that shit was money, too.

*****

"Where the fuck you disappear to? I almost got caught up by that fool Batman," Tone said, replaying the event in his head. "What's so funny?" he asked, while looking at Freddie who was bent over laughing.

"Your fumbling ass, that's what's funny. I watched the whole scene play out, and had I not busted my shit, you would've been caught up. You should've seen the look on them fools' faces when Czod and Jesus almost put hands on their asses." Freddie held up his twin short-nose .357 guns. "I could have laid them bitches to rest, but then I would've had to body shorty who I was standing next to. With lips like hers, I got to get some head from shorty first before I body her."

Both men laughed, knowing things could have gone totally different.

Chapter 6

"Hey, girl," Angel said, greeting Sasha as she entered the room. "It must get lonely out there on that road traveling with those men, huh?" she asked while taking a seat next to her.

"It depends what city we're in and if the malls are up-to-date. Shopping occupies my timme, but there's nothing worse than shopping where the stores are behind on the latest styles."

The two women gave each other a high-five.

Murder smiled. He loved the way Angel and Sasha got along. He knew how well they meshed together would determine how long Angel would be able to stay around.

"You can thank me later," Murder told Sasha.

"Thank you? For what?" Sasha looked at him with a puzzled expression.

"I sent for my baby to come keep you company," he replied, then blew Angel a kiss.

"Oh, I'm baby now, but let me find out you've been fucking with these groupies out here on the road," Angel playfully said, pointing her finger at him.

"For the most part, he seems to be a good boy, Now Stacks is the one who can't seem to keep his dick in his pants. He keeps one or two groupies in his room every night," Sasha said loud enough for Stacks to hear.

"Don't be mad I'm just doing me," he responded, thinking about the two he had last night.

"You see what I'm saying? The boy is terrible. His ass is going to lay down one night with a female who he thinks is named Keisha and wake up to Keith staring him in the face, talking about he enjoyed himself."

The whole room erupted in laughter.

Over the next few weeks, Angel got in where she fit in. She was truly a good look for Murder, but being a seasoned vet and having been around the block a few times, he had to test her loyalty. So, he asked Czucci to shoot his hand to see if she would bite or not. Recognizing the move Murder sent her way, Angel laughed to herself and played accordingly, shooting down every advance while keeping her mouth closed. The reason she decided not to say anything to Murder is because she knew it would have caused conflict between the two or put Murder in a position where he would have to choose between who to believe. Instead, she wanted to prove she could handle herself.

"Out of all the females, why me, Czucci?" Angel asked while applying lip gloss to her full lips. "Especially when you know I'm trying to build something with your boy," she added, turning to face him.

"That ain't my nigga," Czucci responded as he eyed all that ass in her jeans.

"Well, get at a bitch that wants you, because I don't," she said, letting him know he didn't have a chance.

"Yeah, right. Shoot that shit at a nigga that don't know no better." He moved closer to her. "That's why you haven't said anything to your boy about it. You're just waiting on the right opportunity to make your move. But I'm telling you, I won't kiss and tell," he said, wanting to fuck the shit out of her before turning her ass in.

"See, Czucci, what you don't understand is I'm not one of these young dumb bitches who gets blinded by the fame," she told him, removing his hand from her ass. "And regardless of what you were led to believe, not every bitch wants you,"

Angel looked him dead in the eyes to make sure he didn't get it twisted.

"The only reason I haven't told Murder about you is because I'm no damsel in distress who is looking to be rescued. I can hold my own, and the last thing I want to do is cause any friction between my guy and his people. So, I advise you to keep your hands to yourself and grab what's yours. Not what you want to be yours and not what you want to be," Angel added, putting an end to the cat and mouse game.

Czucci left the hotel room liking shorty more than before. He liked how she held up under pressure and didn't get rattled when he pushed down on her.

"Shorty's the truth," he said, catching Murder by the pool. "I pushed down on her and shorty held her own, which is more than I can say about most bitches."

Murder smiled as he thought of the next move he would shoot at her.

*****

"Hey, Rab, you know I talked to them, but you're gonna have to be patient," Tasha B said, looking out of her window.

"Be patient? For what? Tell that muthafucka the change of guards is in the making. Poppa Joe is about to fall from grace, and if he wants to get with the A-team, let's stop playing. Make this happen!" Rab yelled, not feeling that being patient shit.

"Boy, calm down. Shit's gonna happen. Just be ready when it does. He gets a hard-on just thinking about bringing him to his knees, especially after that situation at the Red Zone," Tasha B assured him as she grabbed her blunt out the ashtray.

"He don't have to worry about nothing. My guys and I are going to take care of Poppa Joe. All he—."

"No, Rab!" she yelled, cutting him off. "Poppa Joe is his! If not, y'all will have more problems than you can handle."

Tasha B wanted to make herself clear. Rab listened while trying to figure out how she could speak so freely for Batman like she was running things.

"Hold up, Tasha. You're talking as if you know him or something. I don't know how you're tied in with dude, but whatever you're doing, do your thing. Let's just make this shit happen!" he said, ending the call.

*****

"Where that money at?" Freddie whispered in the man's ear as he tightened the restraints. "You can tell me now or later, but you're going to tell me," he assured him, laughing wickedly.

"Fuck you, faggot motherfuckers!" the female yelled while trying to fight Tone as he tied her up. "Don't tell them nothing," she told her boyfriend, who looked like he was on the verge of breaking.

"Bitch, shut the fuck up!" Tone snapped, then smacked her to get his point across.

"Come on, y'all. Leave her alone. She doesn't have anything to do with this," the man pleaded, breaking his neck to see if his girl was okay.

"Nigga, fuck that bitch. Where that money at?" Freddie asked once more as he pressed his gun against dude's head.

"Hold up, MJ. I think this nigga's more concerned about this bitch than anything else," Tone said, grabbing the girl by her hair. "I bet if I attempt to put this dick in this bitch, he'll be quick to cooperate."

Tone bent her over the couch acting like he was about to do the unthinkable.

"Okay, okay!" the man shouted, not wanting to see his girl get violated. "The money is under the doghouse." Not knowing what was going to happen next, he started sweating bullets. "Take everything, but please don't hurt my girl," he begged, feeling defeated as Freddie went to retrieve the money.

"You soft motherfucker! These faggot-ass niggas don't want no pussy. They would rather fuck you in the ass," the female yelled at her dude, causing Tone to laugh to himself.

Once Freddie returned with the money, he was ready to bounce.

They had found a kilo of heroin along with a hundred grand under the doghouse. Today was definitely a good day.

"Let's ride, playboy," Freddie said, stuffing everything into a duffel bag.

"Yeah, faggot motherfuckers, get the fuck out," the female said, not willing to leave things alone.

"See, bitch, you're gonna make me do something to your sexy ass," Tone said as he grabbed her up. "You act like you want me to fuck you. Call me another faggot!" he challenged, looking her square in the eyes to see how far she wanted to go with this.

The female took a moment to take in her surroundings, looking at her dude, then Freddie, and then at Tone who was standing in front of her. She didn't believe he had the heart to do such a thing.

"You fucking faggot," she spat, testing Tone's gangsta.

Without a moment of hesitation, Tone spun her around, bent her over the couch, and yanked her pants and panties down past her knees.

"Okay then, bitch," he said while pulling his pants down.

The whole time, her dude screamed out for him not to do it.

"Shut the fuck up!" Freddie yelled, then smacked him across the face. "Teach your girl not to run her mouth," he told the dude as Tone penetrated her, then turned back to watch his man beat her pussy up doggie style.

Tied up, dude could only sit there feeling helpless while his girl got pounded. Not wanting to witness his girl being violated, he closed his eyes tightly. Tears began to fall as he tried to block out everything going on around him.

"Call me a faggot now, bitch. Call me one now," Tone said in between each stroke, giving her what she had basically asked for.

In return, she took the dick like a pornstar, throwing the pussy back at him and meeting his thrusts.

"I ain't ducking no rec," she whispered to him over her shoulder.

The excitement of getting fucked during a home invasion had her pussy soaking wet. Not wanting it to end, she slid out of the restraints, grabbed her ass cheeks, and spread them apart so he could dig deeper.

"Yeah, bitch, this what you want?" Feeling his nut tighten, he thrust one last good time before locking up inside her sugar walls. "Yeah, bitch, who's the faggot now?" he said, pulling his dick out of her.

She quickly scrambled to pull her pants up, not giving the semen a chance to drip from her pussy. After gathering herself, she made her way over to her boyfriend who was crying like a little bitch.

"You're the faggot-ass nigga," she spat in disgust and slapped the shit out of him. "You over here crying like you were getting fucked."

Freddie and Tone laughed at her theatrics.

Dude opened his eyes and looked at her in total disbelief. He couldn't believe the woman he loved would disrespect him in such a way.

"I knew you was a tender dick-ass nigga," she said, then looked away. "Tone, kill this weak-ass nigga."

She took the whole room by surprise. Up until that moment, no one's identity had been revealed. Only they knew Tamisha had something to do with the robbery, not the dude who she had befriended and caused to fall in love with her. Regardless of the fact that Tone had on a ski mask, now that she had said his name they couldn't just walk away, .

"Damn, bitch! Why you have to do that?" Tone said, taking off his ski mask.

"Nigga, I know you ain't trippin'," Tamisha replied, looking back and forth between him and Freddie.

"Fuck it. I got him," Freddie jumped in, removing his ski mask, as well.

"No, MJ! Since we all in this together, there's gonna be plenty of times for us to put that work in. Let's see if this bitch is really about that life or is she pretending to be," Tone said while holding out his gun to see if Tamisha would take it.

She didn't hesitate. Fealing fearless, she grabbed the gun and pulled the trigger, causing dude's head to snap back from the impact of the bullet entering his brain. With that, she engraved her position into Tone's life in blood.

*****

"Murder!" Poppa Joe yelled, busting through the door and interrupting everyone's conversation. "We need to shoot down bottom and make things right with ol' boy and them," he said, indicating it was time to reup.

Despite them talking in code, Angel decoded that shit

without blinking an eye. She was slowly putting together her pyramid starting with the boss, to the underbosses and all the way down to the foot soldiers. Outside of this, she was still unsure of a few things. One thing being was Czucci truly the man or just one of Poppa Joe's associates. Until she could confirm or dismiss the notation, she would continue to keep a watchful eye on what was what and who was who.

After Poppa Joe's small talk, everybody began to exit the room, leaving Murder and Angel alone to entertain each other.

"I feel like I'm living a fairytale. I'm Cinderella and you're my Prince Charming. The clock struck midnight, and it's time for me to return back to the life I know now." She kissed him softly and seductively as if it would be their last kiss.

"Never that. The best is yet to come," Murder replied, stealing another kiss. "You will never have to slide up and down another pole other than this one." He placed her hand on his rock-hard dick.

"You so nasty," she said while rubbing his dick the way he liked.

"I don't know where this might lead to, but I do know I like having you around. It seems like you're a keeper. I may be wrong, but only time will tell," Murder expressed, looking deep into her eyes.

"What do you mean you might be wrong?" She poked out her lips as if offended by his words.

"I didn't mean anything bad by it, and I surely don't want you to take it the wrong way. It's just that with the life I live, one cannot afford not to be cautious and must be leary of the company he keeps around because a lot of females fuck with a nigga for all the wrong reasons. A nigga will find himself falling in love with someone who only loves themselves," he stated, hoping she understood.

Angel knew he was pouring his heart out to her, and if it was under different circumstances, she could see herself fucking with a nigga like Murder. However, being she was undercover, she had a job to do. She let it slide in one ear and out the other, but not before hitting him with her hot sixteen.

"I truly feel you and understand you, baby. But, if you allow me to be your escape from life's trials and tribulations, your sun on the cloudy days, and your shelter from the storms, I'll be happy. True enough, we might not know what tomorrow will bring, but let's enjoy today and all that it has to offer. Let's not worry about tomorrow, which may never come. Let's live for today and create lasting memories for our tomorrows." She ended her spill with a kiss of deception.

Lost within a web of lies, Murder couldn't see he was only a pawn in the massive chess game being played by one of the FBI's finest. Angel thrived at her ability to gain one's trust. She just hoped Murder wasn't the type to find himself on his knees blowing out any candles in the middle of the night.

"When it's not even your birthday," she whispered into his ear.

Her words totally threw Murder off. He didn't understand where such a statement came from or what it implied. He didn't pay it much mind, though. Instead, he used it to his advantage.

"Why don't you act like it's my birthday and blow out this candle," he said while pulling at his belt as she seductively licked her lips.

"You know I got you," she told him, playfully smacking his hands out the way as he tugged at his belt.

Chapter 7

"Man, I fuck with shorty that one way," Freddie said, taking the heroin out the press. "She definitely about that life." He examined his work to make sure it looked official.

"Fuck that bitch," Tone replied nonchalantly, thinking about his baby.

It had been two and a half months, and he wished he could lay his eyes on her. He knew like she knew that they both weren't feeling the company the other was keeping, but unlike her, Tone would get gangsta with his and bring a play to whoever he felt was a threat to him getting his baby back.

"That's what your mouth says, but you and I both know we been getting at more money fucking with her these last couple of months than when we were fucking with any of these nigga out here. So, whatever hang-up you got about fucking your girl's bestfriend, put that shit in your back pocket and sit on it," Freddie added, pulling out his phone to make a few moves.

"Whatever," Tone responded even though he knew his man was right.

They were starting to see some real money instead of these twos and fews they were used to getting. He felt his situation was a gift and a curse, being he was getting his weight up and putting himself in a better position to do things for his girl and himself. He was now able to do things he couldn't do before, but at what cost? Sleeping with the enemy and betraying the one he loved?

*****

"That's what I'm talking about, baby. Keep working his ass for information, and I'm telling you, you and the baby are going to be good," Batman assured Tasha B while rubbing her belly.

"I'm going to do my part. I just need you to be careful," she replied sincerely.

Regardless of the financial reward she stood to gain, she had a baby on the way, and the last thing she wanted was for her unborn child to be fatherless.

"I know a lot of these muthafuckas want to see me dead. No matter what, I will try to prevent certain things, but I also know there are some things I have no control over. Just being a police officer puts me in danger because my job is to protect and serve," he said, laughing at his last statement while sliding his hand under her dress. "What can I say, I'm Batman out this bitch."

Wanting to taste her sweet pussy juices, he pulled at her panties.

"Well, we need to protect my dick out there on them streets so you can make it home to serve this pussy," she said, smacking his hands out the way and laying back as she spread her legs. She inserted two fingers inside of her while he watched.

"Why wouldn't I?" he responded, massaging his dick for a moment before removing her fingers so he could lick on her clitoris.

*****

Poppa Joe and his crew finally made it back to the city after handling things with the connect. It would be a few days before the new shipment arrived, so he wanted to hit the town and put on for his city.

"Dig, y'all, we're gonna hit a few spots, go out, and have a good time," Poppa Joe said, entering his baby mansion. "Call up Rab and let him know what's going on," he instructed Murder, then turned to Sasha and put his arms around her waist.

"Normally, I would just be on to the next, but with you, Ms. Lady…" He paused and took a deep breath as if trying to choose his words carefully. "I'm falling for you and I can see myself fucking with you on some exclusive shit if—"

"Shhh!" Sasha put a finger to his lips. "Let's take it one day at a time. I'm having the time of my life, and I don't want you to spoil things with promises and commitments. I'm yours until you show or tell me otherwise," she told him, then kissed him seductively before he had a chance to respond.

Several hours later, they were dressed and ready to hit the town. They hit up all types of spots throughout the city, the crowd tagging along from one club to the next. By the time they headed to the Moonlight, their convoy had grown from a hundred cars to well over three hundred.

Walking to the front of the line like a true boss, Poppa Joe told the staff at the door, "Let them all in. It's on me" Then he blew past security like he owned the club. Once inside, Poppa Joe instantly got into character as if starring in his own self-titled film. *Lights, camera, action!* Poppa Joe wanted all eyes on him as he walked through the maze of people. He stopped a few times to entertain a conversation or two before heading toward the VIP section.

"Stacks, you know what we do!" he yelled out, indicating

he wanted him to buy out the bar.

Sasha stood there watching her boo. It was one thing to be on the outside looking in, but it was something totally different looking from the inside out. She witnessed firsthand day in and day out how Poppa Joe threw away money like he was printing it in a basement.

"That's my shit!" he yelled out as Young Scooter's song "Colombia" blazed through the speakers. He began to recite the lyrics along with the song like he was Young Scooter himself.

Letting Sasha go, he went into his pocket, pulled out a wad of money, and threw the bills into the crowd. That's all it took for the whole crew to begin doing the same as they rapped along with Young Scooter. Sasha laughed to herself while looking into the crowd at the men and women who were trying to figure out how to be a part of Poppa Joe's world. It was all fun until she caught a glimpse of someone from behind that made her heart skip a beat.

"It can't be," she whispered as the person turned around, revealing their identity.

Their eyes locked, and she knew if there were a way to check the person's heartbeat, it would be beating the same as hers. For a moment, time stood still until Poppa Joe grabbed her, interrupting their moment.

"Foreign whip rider when I slide through, but I don't sell dog food. Fill out your application, come to brick school," Poppa Joe rapped, rubbing her backside.

She quickly turned her attention back to where Tone was standing and read his lips.

Don't make me act a fool, he mouthed, then slowly lifted his shirt to slightly expose the butt of his gun.

Immediately, she knew she had to escape, if only for a moment. Meeting up with Tone in the club would be risky being that Poppa Joe's crew was scattered throughtout the place, but the thought of gunplay erupting and innocent people getting caught up was enough for her to throw caution to the wind.

"Girl, are you alright?" Angela asked, noticing the disturbed look on Sasha's face.

"I'm good. I just need to use the restroom," Sasha quickly responded, seeing an opportunity to escape unseen.

Angel had been on top of her game peeping all the people Poppa Joe associated with, including those who he only acknowledged in passing. So, when she noticed Sasha stiffen and her facial expression change, she instantly looked in the direction where Sasha's attention had been drawn. That's when she saw the young gentleman lift his shirt, exposing his gun. At first, she thought about informing Murder of a possible threat, but she decided against it.

"Where did my baby go?" Poppa Joe asked, searching the crowd with his eyes.

"She went to the ladies' room," Angel informed him. "Don't worry, I'm headed there myself. I'll check on her," she told him once she spotted the young gentleman trailing behind Sasha.

Sasha moved through the crowd at top speed. She didn't want to have a confrontation with Tone out in public.

"Seriously, bitch?" Tone barged into the ladies' room right behind her.

Luckily, there were no other women in there, so they had privacy.

"I don't have much time, but please, baby, just trust me with this one," Sasha begged, hoping he would fall back.

"You better tell me something or I'm gonna put so many holes in that nigga they're gonna mistake his ass for a piece of Swiss cheese." He stared at her as if daring her to test his gangsta.

"After everything we've been through, you're going to second guess me now? Just trust me and believe that everything I do, I do for us."

Sasha hoped what she had just said would be enough and that she wouldn't have to go further into detail.

"Sasha—" he began.

"Look, meet me at Shay's around nine-thirty tomorrow morning," she said, cutting him off. "I'll explain everything then. Just know I love you and we'll be better off in the end."

Sasha kissed him on the cheek and made her exit without another word spoken between them. She left out the ladies' room so fast that she never noticed Angel duck out of sight to avoid being seen. Tone exited shortly afterwards, also unaware of Angel's presence. She stood in the shadows trying to digest what she'd overheard and wondering what Ms. Sasha's true intentions were versus what she was portraying them to be.

"I'm going to have to keep a watchful eye on you and this young fellow," Angel whispered to herself, hoping they didn't get in the way of her investigation.

Tomorrow couldn't come fast enough. Tone tossed and turned all night wondering what his baby was up to. He played out different scenarios in his mind but shot each one down.

"My baby ain't built like that," he told himself while getting ready for their breakfast at Shay's.

Anxious to hear what she had to say, he arrived early. Besides, he needed the time to calm his nerves.

"Can I help you?" the waitress asked, pulling out her pen and pad.

Tone looked at his watch. Seeing it was almost nine-thirty, he decided to place an order.

"Let me get an order of French toast, two eggs scrambled with cheese, some home fries, and a glass of OJ." He paused, wondering if he should go ahead and order for Sasha. "Matter of fact, add on an order of banana pancakes, two eggs scrambled with cheese, and another order of home fries."

"If you eat like that all the time, I'd rather clothe you than have to feed you," the waitress replied, causing them both to laugh.

"Naw, I don't get down like that unless I put my meds in

me first," he told the waitress as he handed the menu back to her.

Tone's order arrived before Sasha. So, instead of letting his food get cold, he got his eat on. When he looked up, it was well past ten o'clock.

"I know this bitch ain't play me."

He looked at her order of food across from him growing colder by the minute. The more he looked at it, the more he became upset and the more he wanted to hurt somebody.

"Bitch, I'ma have to send you a message to let you know I'm not playing. Then if you still decide not to get at me, somebody's gonna feel my wrath," Tone whispered to himself as he stood up and dropped a few bills on the table to pay for his food. Then he exited without looking back.

Tone left Shay's on one. He had every intention of sending Sasha a message ASAP to get his point across.

"After all these years, Sasha, you gonna play me like a sucka. Bitch, you got me fucked up!"

Jumping into his BMW X6, Tone drove around the city trying to collect his thoughts while smoking a blunt and wondering what type of message he would send Sasha to let her know he wasn't playing. As he went to put out his blunt in the ashtray, he noticed the inside of vehicle needed a cleaning badly. When he busted a right onto Hudson to hit the self-service carwash, he couldn't believe his luck.

"There has got to be a God somewhere."

Not believing what he stumbled across, his hands began to sweat. He quickly hit the gas pedal and made a right onto Joyce Street, where he parked.

"Yeah, muthafucka, you chose the wrong bitch to lay up with."

Grabbing his ski mask, he tucked his pistol in his waistband and jumped out his truck. Tone then dashed between two houses and hopped the rear fence that led to the alley behind the carwash. Creeping out the alley, he pulled the ski mask down over his face. His target was in sight. It wasn't until the man turned around to put money into the machine that Tone realized he wasn't Poppa Joe.

"Damn," he cursed under his breath.

Even though it wasn't the person who he wanted it to be, Tone continued with his mission.

"Let me get that," Tone said, taking the man by surprise.

The man turned around to find Tone holding a 4.4 Bulldog in his face. However, he seemed to be unfazed while looking down the barrel of the gun.

"You know who you fucking with? Do you know whose car this is?" the man arrogantly said, causing Tone to lose his temper.

"Bitch-ass nigga, do it look like I give a fuck?" Tone replied, then busted off his cannon.

The man screamed in agony, grabbing his leg as he fell back against Poppa Joe's car.

"See, muthafucka, God gave you two ears and one mouth for a reason. Listen more and talk less," Tone said, while relieving him of all his jewelry and searching his pockets. "Now, listen, and listen closely. 'Cause if you don't get this right, I promise you when I catch you again, you won't be walking away. You hear me?"

He waited for the man to respond before continuing.

"Tell Poppa Joe, bad boys ain't no good and good boys ain't no fun. Lord knows she better run off with the right one."

With that, he ran off in the direction he had come from, the whole time laughing because he knew Sasha would be getting at him soon.

*****

"Poppa Joe!" Stacks rushed in the house yelling, interrupting everybody's conversation. "A muthafucka done shot Herdo's leg off!"

"A muthafucka what?" Poppa Joe responded, jumping up.

"They robbed him of his B.H.P chain and everything else he had on him," Stacks added, feeling some type of way because someone had touched one of them.

"The nigga was driving my shit with my initials on the license plate. So, a muthafucka still chose to get at one of mine? Hell naw! Murder, I need you to get on top of this ASAP," Poppa Joe barked, turning his head towards his henchman.

Sasha and Angel sat there with their antennas up as Murder questioned Stacks about what had transpired.

"What he shoot him with?" Murder asked.

"Something that would stop an elephant. He didn't have to do Herdo like that."

Stacks felt bad about his man losing his leg. Then he remembered the message Herdo wanted him to deliver.

"Oh yeah, Poppa Joe, Herdo said the nigga that got at him had a message for you. Something about bad boys ain't no good, good boys ain't no fun, and Lord knows she better run off with the right one. Whatever that's supposed to mean," he said, walking over to the bar to pour himself a drink.

Sasha instantly became nervous. She knew the message was for her and not Poppa Joe. She also knew if she didn't hurry up and reach out to Tone, things would start to spiral out of control and people would be losing more than just their leg.

"You alright?" Angel asked Sasha, seeing the look of worry on her face.

"I'm good. The thought of someone losing their leg got me feeling a little uneasy, that's all." She hoped her facial expression wasn't giving away too much.

"You know, I'm always here if there's anything you want to talk about," Angel threw out there, feeling it was more to the situation than Sasha was letting on.

"Thanks, girl, but I'm good," Sasha replied, then looked Angel straight in her eyes to assure her everything was good.

Not wanting to press the issue, Angel fell back. However,

she continued to replay Herdo's message in her mind, trying to figure out the message within the message. After taking in everything and looking at Sasha, she realized the message wasn't for Poppa Joe, but for Ms. Thang herself.

She better run off with the right one, huh? she thought while smiling to herself.

"You got a helluva dilemma, baby girl, and you better choose the right one or shit's about to get real crazy around here," Angel told Sasha before walking away.

Chapter 8

With the new shipment arriving, Poppa Joe's mind wasn't on anything other than getting to the money. He downplayed Herdo's situation and wrote it off as an isolated incident. While Murder, however, put a fifty-thousand-dollar reward out on the head of whoever got caught wearing Herdo's B.H.P chain. Word traveled fast throughout Columbus; the whole city was on the prowl looking for their man.

"Tone, I know you heard about Herdo. A motherfucker blew his fucking leg off and took his B.H.P chain. Them niggas more concerned about the chain than Herdo's leg, but to each his own," Freddie said shaking his head. "But, let me come across a nigga with that chain. I'm at that fifty grand," he added, causing Tone to laugh.

"Well, get at it then, nigga," Tone said, pulling the chain from inside his shirt and letting it hang in plain sight.

The look on Freddie's face was priceless. It took him a minute to find his voice.

"Nigga, you the one?" he asked, pointing his finger at Tone. "I would've never guessed it was you, but why?"

"Nigga, don't question me. You know how I get down. Anybody can get it!" Tone told him, not wanting to reveal the truth behind his actions.

"True that, fam, but damn! Why put yourself in that type of situation when we getting at enough money to buy a hundred of them damn chains," Freddie said, walking away as he tried to figure it out for himself.

Freddie wasn't the sharpest knife in the drawer, but he damn sure wasn't the dullest either.

"Nigga, you didn't get at dude just to be getting at him. This shit got something to do with Sasha fucking with Poppa Joe, you tender dick-ass nigga." He laughed and pointed his finger at Tone. "And I bet you gave him a message to give to Poppa Joe that only the bitch could decode."

Tone joined in on the laughter.

"Fuck it, fam. You exposed my hand. But, hell, I can still get fifty G's out the deal," Tone responded, holding up Herdo's B.H.P chain.

*****

Despite Herdo's situation, the Brittany Hills niggas ran around the city getting at their money. They acted as if they were above the law and free to sling drugs, blow through red lights, and smoke Cali shit.

Lil' Darryl was coming down Livingston in a rush to hit his lick. Arguing with his baby momma over the phone, he wasn't paying attention and ran a red light.

"Fuck!" he yelled out once he saw po-po pull tight behind him. "Bitch, let me call you back."

Ending the call, he hoped they were after someone else. But, his worst nightmare came true when they turned on their disco lights, indicating they were in fact pulling him over. Looking in his rearview mirror, he felt a bit relieved to see it was a female officer. He decided to play it safe being that he only ran a red light and had a valid driver's license with proof of insurance.

"Do you know why I pulled you over?" the female officer asked once she approached the car.

"I ran that red light back there," he replied, trying not to sound too ghetto as he reached to retrieve his license and insurance card.

"Not only that, but you were doing thirty-five miles per hour in a twenty-five." the officer added as she looked at the young man behind the wheel of such an expensive car.

Not new to the force, she figured him to be involved in the same type of illegal activities as most young men who drove those types of cars, but that wasn't her concern.

"Don't worry; as long as all your documents check out, I'll just write you a warning and you can be on your way," she said, then started walking back to her cruiser.

Out of nowhere, Batman pulled up, blocking Lil' Darryl from being able to pull off.

"Officer Johnson, what do we have here?" Batman yelled out as he exited his SUV.

"It's nothing, Batman. Just a minor traffic stop," Officer Johnson responded as she opened the door to her cruiser.

Seeing Batman on the scene, Lil' Darryl's nerves began to get the best of him. His heart started beating so fast that it felt like it was about to jump out his chest. Then he noticed Big Country pull up and jump out. Before he could decide what to do, Big Country had snatched him out his car.

"Lil' Darryl, you've been a very busy dude," Big Country said, searching him. Then he rushed inside Batman's SUV while another vice officer jumped into Lil' Darryl's car.

"What the fuck is going on, Batman?" Officer Johnson inquired as she watched both vehicles peel off into traffic.

"Don't worry, Officer Johnson. It's for his own protection. I'm giving him a chance to help himself or go to jail. You know how we work." He reached to take Darryl's license and insurance card from her hand.

"That I do, and I better not hear anything bad happened to that young man either," she warned while getting into her cruiser.

"Don't worry; I got him," he told her, jumping into Big Country's SUV.

It didn't take long for Batman to get to the substation

where they were holding Lil' Darryl.

"Y'all don't have anything on me. My lawyer is going to eat this shit up," Lil' Daryl assured them as if he had nothing to worry about.

Just then, Batman walked into the room and started taking pictures of Lil' Darryl sitting at the round table talking with Big Country and two other vice officers.

"What the fuck you doing?" Lil' Darryl questioned, unaware of Batman's intentions.

Without saying a word, Batman sat down at the computer and printed out the pictures he had taken.

"Lil' Darryl, tell me how you like these," he said, throwing the pictures down on the table in front of him. "What would your daddy Poppa Joe think of these?" he added, laughing.

Lil' Darryl knew the pictures didn't look good, regardless if they were innocent or not.

"It looks like you're at the round table with some true bosses," Big Country added, seeing an opportunity to get in on the conversation.

Lil' Darryl began to sweat from nervousness. He didn't know what type of game they were playing or what they intended to do with the pictures.

"Stop playing, Batman! I'm not trying to get killed over no bullshit-ass pictures. I know y'all found the two bricks of cocaine, so charge me and take me downtown," Lil' Darryl demanded, ready to take his charges like a man.

Batman started laughing before revealing more pictures he knew would get a reaction out of him. "If that's what you want, I have no problem doing so, but before I do, I want you to take a good look at these."

Batman threw down another set of pictures in front of him. As Lil' Darryl flipped through the pictures, his eyes grew large.

"No, Batman! No!" He looked at the pictures in disbelief. "He wouldn't do me like that. He wouldn't stab me in the heart knowing how I feel about my baby momma," Lil' Darryl cried while looking at the pictures that displayed betrayal of the two people who he trusted the most.

"It is what it is, Lil' Darryl. You can either allow Poppa Joe to continue fucking you and your baby momma, or you can start fucking them back and fuck Poppa Joe in the ass with no vaseline." Batman paused to allow everything time to sink in. "The choice is yours," he added, waiting on Lil' Darryl to make his decision.

"What I need to do?" Lil' Darryl finally replied while still staring at the pictures.

"Good choice," Batman said, patting him on the shoulder and then dropping his keys into his lap. "Welcome to the winning team."

Batman loved how his perfect plan was playing out. Poppa Joe wouldn't know what hit him.

*****

"I see you're good at what you do," Officer Johnson said to his partner as he reviewed the report she had just submitted to her superiors.

"Why wouldn't I be? This is the job I was born to do. I've witnessed firsthand the destruction drugs cause within the community, how it can pit a family against one another. I've seen mothers pimp their own flesh and blood, whether it be their daughters or sons. Not only that, but I've experienced abuse from my own family members, including uncles who were under the influence or just plain sick in the mind and thought it was okay to sneak into my room at night. So, hell yeah, I'm good at what I do," she said, giving her partner a peek inside her childhood.

"I didn't know it was so personal," he said.

"Oh, it's not," she responded, closing the folder. "When you allow things to get personal, it affects your ability to think and see things clearly. I can't afford either. I'm out here putting my life on the line, rubbing shoulders with killers and drug dealers who won't think twice to kill me if my true identity is ever discovered." She stood up and looked her partner in his eyes. "Now, if you will excuse me, I have work to do," she added, leaving him standing there with a shocked look on his face.

*****

"What it do?" Tone said, answering his phone withouth bothering to check the Caller ID.

"You didn't have to do that," the caller responded, causing Tone's heart to skip a beat.

Hearing his baby's voice, the phone slipped from his hand and fell between the door and his seat. While trying to quickly retrieve it, he almost crashed into a parked car.

"Hello…hello," Sasha said after receiving no response.

"Sasha!" he yelled into the phone, pulling over before he killed himself.

"Yes, baby, it's—"

"Fuck all that. Where you at? I'm coming to get you," Tone demanded. He wasn't trying to hear anything else.

"Look, baby, I'm calling you because I don't want you to get caught with that chain," she said, feeling she was doing the right thing.

"You calling me about a goddamn chain! Seriously, Sasha?"

Tone could feel his temperature rising, and he was ready to turn up for real.

"Please, just calm down and allow me to put us in a better position. I know you think I'm trying to play you, but I'm not. You have to trust me and believe that what we have is realer than life itself," she continued, pouring out her heart.

Tone listened as she said all the things he wanted to hear, but what she had yet to say is what she was up to exactly.

"I hear all that. If nothing else, I trust you and believe in what we have. But, what the fuck does all that got to do with you being with that nigga?"

He waited for the answer to the one question that would shine light on everything.

"Not over the phone," she said, hoping he would leave it at that.

"What the fuck you mean, not over the phone? You stand me up; I don't hear from you until now, and the one question I need an answer for, you won't tell me shit. Bitch, don't make me come out there," he threatened, pulling back into traffic.

"I can't win with you! You're quick to throw that love and loyalty shit in my face when it suits you and what you're trying to do. But, the first time I ask you for the same shit in return and need you to fall back, it's a problem. Now tell me where's the trust, where's the love, and where the fuck is the loyalty? Huh, Tone?" she said, giving him the chance to response but thinking he would only argue that her situation was different than his.

However, Tone was boxed in. He knew he had to fall back and allow things to play out even though he didn't want to.

"Dig," he said, then paused to collect his thoughts. "I'm not liking this shit one bit, especially with you laid up with that nigga, but being that I love your punk ass, I will give you a chance to do this for us. The next time you stand me up, though, I'ma have more than a bunch of these chains. On that note, love is love even when it hurts," Tone told her, ending their call before he changed his mind.

*****

"What up, Misha?" Freddie said, opening the door for Tamisha.

"You tell me," she said, making her way inside. "Where's your boy? He ain't answering my calls. What's up with that?"

She turned to face Freddie, looking for an answer as he shut the door.

"I don't know where his gay ass is. He probably somewhere getting in touch with his feminine side," Freddie said, laughing as he looked Tamisha up and down, loving the way those jeans were fitting her.

"I see you got jokes. Seriously, I have a play I'm trying to put down, and I need to know if he's with it or not," she said as she pulled out her phone to call him again.

"Fuck if that nigga's with it or not. I'm all about the paper," he let Tamisha know.

"I'm all about the paper, too," Tone said, catching everybody by surprise as he stood in the doorway to the kitchen.

"You been in the kitchen all this time?" Tamisha asked, looking back and forth between him and Freddie.

"Naw, Misha, I just came through the back door and commented on what I heard," he responded while taking a seat.

"Well, this is the situation," Tamisha continued. "One of your niggas who I know you fuck with got at me. He exposed his hand and I'm trying to take him up top," she informed them, not trying to sugarcoat anything.

Tone sat back listening as she continued telling them how she wanted to get at Chin.

"What you think?" Tone asked, directing his question at Freddie while passing Tamisha the blunt.

"You already know I'm with it," Freddie said.

"Well, I'm not," Tone said, surprising everyone with his decision. He stood up. "That shit is like somebody asking me to get at Freddie. It's rules to this shit, and even though some rules are made to be broken, I'm not willing to bend, fold, or break with this one. You feel me?"

Tone looked both of them in their eyes before turning to leave.

"That shit sounds good," Tamisha responded, causing

Tone to stop in his tracks.

"What the fuck is that supposed to mean?"

"You probably do fuck with dude, but let him tell it, you ain't his nigga."

Her words caused Freddie to choke on his blunt from laughing so hard.

"Niggas quick to safeguard a muthafucka when that same muthafucka is sneak dissing behind a nigga's back," she added.

Tone started getting heated. Just as he was about to ask what Chin had said, he caught himself. He knew Tamisha was trying to manipulate him just so they could hit the lick.

"Whatever the nigga said or didn't, he gets a pass on the strength, just like you would Freddie." Then he pulled out Herdo's chain. "Some niggas don't, though."

He hoped Tamisha got the point.

The room was silent as Tone walked out the room.

"He's the one who shot off Herdo's leg?" Tamisha turned to Freddie, expecting him to answer.

"You better believe it," Freddie responded while taking the last hit of the blunt.

Chapter 9

"Columbus P.D.!" Batman and his crew yelled as they raided one of Poppa Joe's stash spots in the middle of the night. The scene they stumbled upon shocked them all.

"What the fuck!" Batman couldn't believe his eyes.

There in the bed was a frightened Shamar cuddled up with another man.

"Bring your gay ass here."

Batman snatched Shamar up by his long braids and dragged him from the bedroom, down a flight of stairs, and all the way into the kitchen.

"Tie this bitch up," he instructed one of the vice cops as Big Country walked his boyfriend into the kitchen. "Tie his ass up, too."

Batman shook his head in disgust while looking at both of them.

"I have to give it to you, Shamar. You're more of a bitch than I thought you were."

He ordered his team to search the place while the two men sat there tied up.

Shamar trembled with fear. He wasn't afraid of going to jail, though; he was more concerned about his secret being revealed.

"Look, Batman, I'll tell you whatever you want to know, but please, leave this between us," he begged, hoping to save his gangsta.

"The place is clean," Big Country told Batman, interrupting Shamar's pleading.

"That ain't right," Batman responded, turning to Shamar. He knew the money and drugs were hidden within the walls or a safe built within the house. "I don't have all day. Where's that shit?" he said, grabbing a hand full of Shamar's braids and jerking his head back.

"I'll tell you everything. Just don't tell nobody about my people," Shamar said, trying to make a deal with Batman.

"I told you that I don't have all day." Growing impatient, Batman turned to Shamar's boyfriend and laced him with two shots to the head.

"Noooo!" Shamar cried out, seeing his lover killed right in front of him. "You didn't have to do that, Batman! You didn't have to—"

"Shut the fuck up, faggot motherfucker. You know the game we play. Either you tell me where that shit is or I'm going to fuck you in the ass with every broom, mop, and bottle that I can find in this bitch. Now, stop wasting my time. Where's that shit?" Batman demanded, looking at Shamar like he was seconds away from doing what he claimed he would do.

Shamar hung his head low to his chest, feeling lost because his lover was dead. Finally, he told Batman everything he wanted to know. While Batman kept Shamar company, Big Country and the other three officers quickly went to retrieve the goods.

"You could have prevented this," Batman said, pointing to Shamar's lover on the floor. "This wasn't the plan, but what's done is done. We can't turn back now."

"We good!" Big Country told Batman, then instructed the others to load up the SUV's.

Batman acknowledged his partner while continuing his conversation with Shamar.

"I wish I could trust you, Shamar, but—"

"Yes, yes, you can, Batman. I swear you can. I'll clean this shit up and get rid of everything," Shamar said, hoping he could convince him.

"I wish it was that simple," Batman said as he poured gasoline over Shamar's lover. "I wish it didn't have to come to this." Turning, he poured gasoline on Shamar, as well.

Shamar became hysterical, screaming like a bitch.

"No, Batman! Please!" He pleaded in between screams terrified of what he knew was about to go down.

Big Country could hear Shamar's cries from outside. So, he quickly rushed inside to shut him up by duct taping his mouth closed. Batman continued to pour gasoline everywhere.

"There's casualties of war and you just happen to be one. Now don't take this personal, Shamar, but I never liked your bitch ass anyway."

He struck a match and held it close to Shamar, who was twisting and turning trying to free himself.

"See you in hell, faggot motherfucker," Batman said, dropping the match onto his gasoline-soaked body.

He exited the house with a deranged look on his face like he was Lucifer himself.

Thinking about the two burning corpses left inside, he whispered, "Columbus on fire."

*****

Several hours later, Poppa Joe was awakened by the non-stop ringing of his phone.

"What!" he yelled into his phone, knowing it better be one hell of a reason his line was blowing up early in the morning. "Get the fuck out of here! You get every muthafucka out here ASAP. I don't give a fuck what time it is. You wake the muthafuckas up."

He threw his phone across the room.

Sasha woke up from the noise. She watched Poppa Joe as

he paced back and forth while cursing himself under his breath. Then he walked onto his balcony in the master bedroom. Curious to know what was going on, she slid out the bed to join him on the balcony. Without saying a word, she began massaging his shoulders, neck, and every place she felt tightness in his body. Poppa Joe allowed her to work her magic, surrendering himself under her touch. He needed to clear his mind in order to think clearly before jumping to conclusions.

"Damn, that shit feels good," he commented as he felt the tension leaving his body.

"Baby, I don't know what's going," Sasha whispered in his ear while still massaging his back. "But, logic and anger are like water and oil; they just don't mix. If you're trying to see things clearly and not behind smoke screens of lies and deception, you have to focus and never allow emotions to supersede your intelligence," she added, kissing him on the back of his neck before turning to walk back inside.

To him, he felt she spoke from a place of concern, but what she was really doing was trying to pick him for information without actually coming out and asking him.

He felt like she was the perfect fit for his life. All the heartache, pain, and disappointment he had experienced in past relationships suddenly seemed worth it. He believed he now had something better with Sasha than he'd ever had when dealing with the opposite sex.

"Someone robbed and burned down one of my stash spots, leaving two bodies behind," he revealed, giving Sasha the information she was seeking.

She didn't respond. Instead, she placed her head against his chest, knowing when to be vocal and when to listen. She remembered what Tone would always tell her. *God gave you two ears and one mouth for a reason. Listen more and talk less.*

Moments later, everyone arrived and took a seat in the dining room around the massive table as they waited on

Poppa Joe to enter the room. Rab and KC whispered amongst themselves. Lil' Darryl sat in a chair trembling like a leaf, hoping his betrayal would go unnoticed. As he watched Murder and Stacks conversing, his hands began to sweat and his nerves started to jump. Then the moment arrived when Poppa Joe entered the room accompanied by his two German Rottweilers, David and Goliath. They ran through the room growling at Rab, KC, and Lil' Darryl.

"Watch them, boys. Watch them," Poppa Joe egged his dogs on, seeing the look on the men's faces.

"Come on now, Poppa Joe. Get these crazy-ass motherfuckers before they bite something," Rab said, not feeling the vibe of things.

"If you sit your ass still and don't make any sudden movements, you got no problems. Otherwise, you might have something to worry about," he said, circling the table while keeping his attention on Rab, KC, and Lil' Darryl, the only three people outside of him, Murder, and Stacks who knew about the stash house.

"As we speak, I'm waiting on the dental records because I know Shamar could be hightailing it out of town with my shit by now. I have my people in Cincinnati on the lookout for his ass, though." He glared at KC and Rab, knowing that was their boy. "I'm giving a muthafucka a chance to come forward now with any information that might be of interest to me, because as soon as the sun rises, I'm gonna get to the bottom of this. And when I do, it's going to be hell to pay."

Poppa Joe stopped directly behind KC and Rab. David and Goliath, sensing tension in the air, began growling at the two men. Murder commanded them to leave the room because they were ready to kill.

"I know you're feeling some type of way about the spot being hit, but—"

"But nothing, motherfucker," Poppa Joe responded, cutting KC off. "You think I want to hear anything else besides what happened to my spot?" he added, pulling out his long-nose .357 and pointing it directly at him. "You think I want to hear the bullshit you trying to shoot to me? You think…" He grabbed KC by the back of his head and forced the barrel of the gun inside his mouth. "Motherfucker, I'll blow your fucking brains out and won't think twice about it!"

Seeing the look on his man's face, Murder sensed things were about to get real ugly fast.

"No! Poppa Joe, no! It ain't worth it. Let me do my job and unravel what the fuck is going on before we bring a play to anybody."

Murder was trying to calm his man down before he did something he might regret later.

Poppa Joe loosened his grip as he slowly removed the barrel out of KC's mouth. He knew killing him without solid proof would be a little extreme, but he needed to make a point. Just as quick as he put his pistol away, he opened a butterfly knife, swirling it in the air until the blade appeared.

"Yo' bitch ass better not have anything to do with this," he said, then plunged the knife into KC's hand with brutal force.

"Ahhhhh!" KC yelled out in agonizing pain. He desperately tried to pull the knife out of his hand and the table as Poppa Joe exited the room.

Everyone was in total shock except Murder. He took the opportunity to sit back and observe Rab, KC, and Lil' Darryl's reactions, hoping to detect betrayal through their body language. Stacks, on the other hand, found the whole episode to be hilarious.

"Damn! Poppa Joe just Nino Browned your ass," he said, laughing as he watched KC wrap his hand up.

Despite Stacks making light of the situation, true enough there were a G-money and Pookie in the room, and the longer they went undetected, things were definitely going to get worse.

*****

A couple days later, the dental records confirmed the identity of the two burned corpses found inside Poppa Joe's stash house. The streets were buzzing trying to connect the dots as to how Boomer, a known gay, ended up being one of the dead bodies. Some believed Boomer was living a double life, doing hair in the day and secretly slanging his thang at night to paying customers of the gay inner circle.

"I'm telling you, Murder, fuck what they saying. Boomer and Shamar were lovers, and it's a shame," Bink told Murder.

This news took Murder by surprise. Out of all the different scenarios, Murder never would have guessed they were lovers.

"Good looking out, Bink. I swear you put me onto something. I would've never come up with that."

He broke Bink off a few dollars for sharing that bit of information with him. Murder left adding that information with all the other information he'd been gathering over the past couple of days. He was content with the things he was able to uncover and ready to report back to Poppa Joe. But first, he decided he would pull down on Myron, a wannabe gangster who swore he had something important to share with him.

Before Murder could make it back to let Poppa Joe know his findings, Rab was in Poppa Joe's ear telling him about Lil' Darryl.

"How you come about this information?" Poppa Joe asked, thinking Rab was trying to throw his man under the bus.

"This bitch that I fuck with saw him get pulled over and Batman whisked him away. She been trying to get at me—" Rab immediately stopped talking when Murder entered the room.

"Hold up, Rab," Poppa Joe said. "This muthafucka is claiming Lil' Darryl—"

"Yeah, Poppa Joe, ole boy's fucking with the enemy,"

Murder confirmed. "But that's the least of our worries," he added, ready to reveal something he knew would surely cause a war.

"What are you getting at?" Poppa Joe responded.

"We're gonna have to change everything up. If Lil' Darryl told him about the spot, who knows what else he told him. We got to believe everything is compromised and change shit up immediately," Murder said, letting Poppa Joe know the seriousness of things.

Poppa Joe grew irate thinking back to how Lil' Darryl was acting during the meeting. He couldn't believe he misread the obvious sign of betrayal, especially with the way he was shaking.

"I want that bitch's head and I want it ASAP. I raised that motherfucker, and this is how he repays me? This is how you repay a motherfucker who has shown you nothing but love?"

Poppa Joe shook his head while trying to make sense of it all.

"And that motherfucker got my man killed," Rab said, trying to add fuel to the fire.

"Hell, your man wasn't all he claimed to be," Murder replied, ready to expose Shamar's gay ass.

"What the fuck is that supposed to mean?" Rab responded, ready to defend his boy.

"Fuck all that tongue-wrestling shit. We got bigger issues on our hands," Poppa Joe said, interrupting them.

"That we do, but I'm not about to let Murder or anyone else shoot shots at my man like he wasn't a stand-up dude," Rab said, turning his attention back to Murder.

"Stand-up dude or not, it still doesn't excuse the fact that he liked bending over to pick up soap while a muthafucka stood behind him," Murder retorted, revealing Shamar's secret. "Him and Boomer were lovers. That's the reason Boomer was in the spot, 'cause he damn sure wasn't there to do no hair," Murder continued, spreading the icing on the cake.

"Fuck you, Murder!" Rab shouted, ready to get it popping.

"Naw, nigga. Fuck ya man. He's the one taking dick," Murder shot back, wishing Rab would jump out there.

Poppa Joe became fed up with listening to the bullshit. "Y'all fussing back and forth about if the nigga was gay or not. Is y'all serious?" He threw a vase across the room, shattering it against the wall. "I want Batman and Lil' Darryl's heads! And if y'all can't handle that, I'll find someone who can," he said, then left them to digest his words.

Rab stormed out of Poppa Joe's house hotter than a firecracker. His blood pressure was through the roof, and if he didn't have a play in motion to get rid of them both, he would've shot them where they stood, especially Murder's bitch ass.

"I'ma handle you myself," he told himself, then placed a call to Tasha B to set up a meeting with Batman.

Within an hour, he was standing face to face with Batman.

"Calm down. I didn't know he was a part of the A-team. You can't hold me accountable for something I wasn't aware of," Batman said, trying to smooth things over.

"What's done is done," Rab simply replied, looking at the bigger picture. "Dig, Batman, I think it's best if we move forward and get rid of Poppa Joe. He's getting beside himself. I just left him and you won't believe what type of shit he's on."

"Fuck Poppa Joe and what he's on! His days are numbered, believe me," Batman assured him. "You just be ready to take over when it's time," he added with a broad smile.

"Oh yeah, and if you need help moving that work, I got you," Rab offered, referring to the thirty bricks they took from Poppa Joe's stash house.

"Being that you mentioned it, I'm gonna have Big

Country drop that off to you. I know those things going for forty G's, but I'ma hit your hand at thirty G's."

Batman knew Poppa Joe wasn't letting him eat at that price.

"Hell, if you playing fair like that, I can put you onto a few more of Poppa Joe's spots."

Rab loved doing business with Batman already.

*****

"These soft muthafuckas ain't about this life!" Poppa Joe screamed.

Everybody had left long ago.

"I need to pull up these niggas' skirts and expose the panties they wearing," he vented while throwing things and knocking stuff over.

Sasha sat back and allowed him to rant until he calmed down a bit. She waited until the right moment to shoot her move.

"Baby, let me help you."

Her offer took him by surprise.

"Don't look at me like that!" she said, seeing the way he was looking at her. "I told you from the beginning it's more to me than—"

"No, baby. What type of man would I be if I allowed my girl to get involved?" he said cut, not trying to entertain the conversation anymore.

"That's your problem. You're quick to judge a book by its cover and get fooled everytime. You're so smart that you're dumb. You will step over a dollar to pick up a penny; all because you didn't pay close attention to the details and you think you know every fucking thing," Sasha spat, showing Poppa Joe another side to her.

Poppa Joe playing her words over in his head. Never in his life had he been complimented and disrespected at the same time.

"Okay, lil' momma, pump your brakes. You made your point." Recognizing Sasha had some nigga tendencies in her. "Now tell daddy what you got going on in your little mind."

He gave her the opportunity to lay out her moves.

Sasha didn't hesitate putting everything into prospective using different metaphors to get her point across.

"Life is like a game of chess, and there shouldn't be one person within the crew who feels irreplaceable. Every piece on the board is expendable, even your queen when it comes to protecting the king. I'm not taking anything from Murder or anyone else on your team, but they have lost their edges. They are not money hungry anymore, leaving room for complacency. And when that happens, niggas start shying away from war, making you vulnerable to be touched."

Sasha paused to see if she was getting through to him. Then she shot Poppa Joe different propositions on how he should shake things up.

"The best way to make a person do their job is to get someone else to do it for them. Once they feel their job is in jeopardy, they will fight like hell to keep it."

Poppa Joe listened closely. He loved what he heard, because what she spoke was the truth. He couldn't deny the complacency within his crew, and the more he thought about it the more he realized it was time to shake things up.

"Okay, baby, tell me more about your people that can get the job done," he said, becoming more interested in putting his team on edge.

"My people are a bunch of hungry young lions who are looking for an opportunity to show their worth and get down with someone like you. You better believe we have something beautiful in the making," Sasha said with a smile.

"Okay, baby, get at your people and put them on Lil' Darryl's ass. I'll let you know about that other situation depending on how they handle this one."

He looked at Sasha in a different light now. Her thought process was unlike any other female that he had ever come across.

"Damn, I love you," he whispered, not meaning for Sasha to hear him.

"I do, too," she replied.

Her response made him think she was implying she loved him, but she was really saying she loved herself, too. When caught up in the moment, it is common for people to have selective hearing. Poppa Joe heard what he wanted to hear versus what she had actually said.

Chapter 10

"What's wrong?" Angel asked Murder as he slid out the bed. "Whatever it is, it's written all over your face."

"Is it that obvious?" he replied, rubbing his face with both hands.

"It is!" Seeing it as an opportunity for her to press forward, she slid out of the bed and stood right behind him. "If we plan on building something together, we have to open up to one another and not be afraid of expressing our fears. We have to trust each other and know that we won't pass judgement," she said, wrapping her arms around him.

Murder turned to face her and hugged her back. He loved how she felt in his arms. The walls he had built to shield his inner feelings began to crack.

"It's hard to reveal a side of me that has never been exposed. My name is Murder for a reason; that's all I've done my whole life." He paused to see if she read into what he was saying. "I lived on the edge where I put my life and freedom on the line. Running from police felt like I was dancing with the devil and getting away was like escaping from hell," he continued, sharing his inner feelings and thoughts.

Angel smiled inside while listening intently to everything being said. This was the moment she'd been patiently waiting for, the moment where he felt comfortable to share everything.

"I'm not feeling this shit anymore. I'm not a teenager with nothing to lose." He released her and walked over toward the nearest window. "I never imagined I would live to see my eighteenth birthday, let alone be standing here twenty something years later. I'm a grown-ass man with dreams; I'm financially stable." He turned to face her again. "I want kids. I want someone I can call my own."

"So what's stopping you? What's holding you back from getting those things that you want?" she asked, egging him on.

Murder stood on the edge of deciding whether to stand firm, fall, or jump off that cliff headfirst revealing the untold truth. He looked at Angel and saw the female who he wanted to call his own, the woman he wanted to bear his kids, the person he felt he could trust.

Then he blurted out, "Poppa Joe wants me to kill Batman."

*****

"Four, five, six, muthafucka!" Tone yelled, picking up the bank off the ground in a c-low game. "I'm only putting two hundred in the bank," he said, pocketing the rest of the money as he smiled while looking at all the sad faces around him.

"Why are you going to break the bank down like that?" DJ protested, hoping Tone would add some more money to it.

"Because I can," Tone told him bluntly. He watched a few get mad and take off up the street.

"Niggas kill me. They start getting a little money and want to start acting brand new," RJ mumbled under his breath.

"Come on, RJ. Bitches whisper, men speak their mind, and faggots shut the fuck up," Tone provoked. "Now the question is, which one are you trying to be?"

At that moment, everything became intense. The wrong response, movement, or gesture could result in some serious repercussions. Before RJ could do any of those, a black BMW with smoked-out windows crept down the block, drawing everyone's attention. Many reached for their guns once the BMW pulled up and sat idle with its engine still running.

"What it do?" Tone said, answering his phone but never taking his eyes off the unfamiliar BMW.

"Are you going to stand there and mean mug or come parlay with me?" asked the female on the other end of the phone.

Tone's facial expression changed and his heart began beating rapidly. He almost couldn't breath.

"Sasha?" he whispered, finding it hard to believe she was only a few feet away.

Not waiting for a response, he allowed his heart to guide him, ending their call. Once he was within inches of the car, he heard the doors unlock. He opened the door and there she was. If time could stand still, nothing in the world would've mattered to him but that moment.

"'Bout time you showed up. I was beginning to think love don't live here no more," he said, sliding into the car.

"Never that," Sasha replied and then pulled off into traffic, leaving niggas standing there curious to know who was behind the tint.

As she sped down 4th Street heading towards Franklin Park, she glanced back and forth between the road and the love of her life. She was so consumed with her thoughts that she never noticed a gray Magnum with tinted windows following right behind her.

"So what's the deal, Sasha? You sucking and fucking that nigga for what?" Tone asked, breaking the silence.

"And you sucking and fucking my girl for what?" she shot back. "I wasn't even trying to go there, but if this is what you want, we can go there."

She was ready to go blow for blow with him.

"The difference between me and Mish is we getting

money together, unlike you and dude."

He wasn't going to admit that he was fucking her girl.

"You and that bitch are that comfortable around each other that y'all got pet names for each other?" She shook her head, not wanting to believe he would betray her like that.

"Miss me with all that, Sasha." He wasn't feeling how she was coming at him. "You quick to accuse me of fucking your girl, when you the one laid up in that nigga's bed every night. Then you want to rock me to sleep with all this 'doing it for us' shit. You the only one benefiting from this shit, because I damn sure ain't seen one red cent."

He broke it down from his point of view rather than the one she would have liked him to believe. Sasha could hear the uncertainty in his voice as she pulled into Franklin Park and looked for the perfect place to park.

"That's why I'm here," she said, then reached in her bag and threw twenty bands in his lap.

*****

After returning back to the hood, Tone didn't know how to digest what Sasha had shared with him. He didn't know if he was being used as a pawn or if his baby was really trying to put them in a position to leave this life behind. The twenty bands to do Lil' Darryl was like giving a fat kid a piece of cake. He was going to eat that up without a second thought, but killing a police officer was something totally different.

"What the fuck is wrong with you?" Freddie asked, seeing the puzzled look on his man's face. "You missing Boomer, too?" he added, trying to sneak a joke in.

"Naw, nigga! Not as much as your gay ass do," Tone responded, looking at Freddie sideways.

"What, you on your period or something?" he said, seeing Tone wasn't in a playing mood.

Tone didn't respond right away. He was deep in thought trying to figure out how he would present the situation to

Freddie.

"If a muthafucka offered you a half a mill to touch somebody in the city, who wouldn't you touch?"

He threw it out there to see how Freddie would respond.

"Nigga, for a half a mill, Mom dukes can get it," he responded, wondering where Tone was headed with this conversation.

"Seriously, nigga, who wouldn't you touch?"

He wasn't trying to hear what Freddie had just told him.

"Seriously, my ass. Mom Dukes can get it for a half a mill. Hell, she's already lived her life. She might as well—"

"Nigga, shut the fuck up with that shit," Tone said, cutting him off. He knew damn well Freddie wouldn't do such a thing. "But since it's laying like that, a muthafucka got a half a mill to kill Batman right now."

He tried to read the expression on Freddie's face.

"Nigga, I don't give a fuck if it was the president. If I said Mom Dukes, that means anybody can get it," Freddie stated, letting it be known where he stood.

Tone looked at his man. He knew once he committed to killing Batman, there was no turning back.

"You right. For half a mill, anybody *can* get it. But, first, we got to handle this other situation before we get the green light on Batman's punk ass," Tone told him.

"We ain't did it yet? What the hell are we waiting for?" Freddie responded, not playing about getting that half a mill.

*****

After the situation with Shamar, Lil' Darryl had been spending more time with his grandma, allowing her to use him as she pleased.

"Boy, stop complaining and set the garbage on the curb!" she yelled from the kitchen.

"Damn, Grandma, I don't know how one person can accumulate so much garbage in a week. I swear you got your girls dropping their trash off before y'all go to bingo on Wednesday nights. This shit doesn't make no sense," Lil' Darryl complained as he dragged the last of the trash cans to the curb.

"Boy, you better stop all that cussing around here. You're not too old to get your mouth washed out with soap," she threatened while checking her pot of greens of the stove. "Now, let me hear one more curse word."

Lil' Darryl finished doing what he was told without allowing another curse word to escape his lips.

"She would love that," he said to himself, then laughed at the thought of his mouth being washed out with soap.

It had been two weeks since Lil' Darryl chose to roll over on Poppa Joe, and he couldn't wait until Batman delivered on his promise.

I can't wait until his ass is dead or locked the fuck up.

Those were the two things Lil' Darryl wished upon Poppa Joe. True enough, Poppa Joe was wrong for fucking his bitch, but his bitch was just as wrong. Still, he held Poppa Joe solely accountable for their betrayal.

"Boy, you better not light that reefer in my house," his grandmother said, sneaking up on him while he was rolling up. "You better take that outside somewhere," she added before making her way upstairs.

Lil' Darryl didn't put up an argument. He just went out on the front porch. He was so consumed with his own thoughts that he didn't notice the mailman placing the mail in the neighbor's mailbox next door.

"That sure does smell good," the mailman commented while standing on the neighbor's porch.

"Shit, you can hit this if you want to," Lil' Darryl offered, taking another hit of his blunt.

"I wish I could." The mailman walked across the grass holding mail in his hand. "But the last thing I need is to lose my job. My girl wouldn't understand."

He carefully made his way up the steps of Lil' Darryl's

grandmother's porch.

"When you start letting the lady of the house dictate your shit, you will be forever second-guessing your next move," the mailman continued, acting as though he was an expert on relationships.

When the mailman reached where Lil' Darryl was seated, he took the blunt and handed him the mail. "Fuck it," the postal worker said, getting his smoke on.

It wasn't until Lil' Darryl noticed the mail he was holding didn't belong to his address that he grew leary. Then he turned to see mail already in the mailbox.

"Did the mailman already come?" he asked, looking puzzled as he pointed to the mail in the mailbox.

"Yes, but he forgot to deliver this…"

With those words, the mailman rocked Lil' Darryl's world with two shots to his chest. The impact of the bullets knocked him out of his chair. There was no sound of gunfire. With a look of disbelief, he held his hands over his wounds.

"Poppa Joe said you should've known better."

The mailman pumped two more shots into his body before stepping over him and grabbing the mail he had given him to hold.

"Damn, this is some good shit," Freddie said, hitting the blunt once more before making his escape.

Chapter 11

Once news of Lil Darryl's death reached Rab, he was furious. He couldn't believe Murder would be that thirsty to touch him at his grandmother's house. Enraged, he rushed over to Poppa Joe's house. No sooner than he pulled up, Murder exited his car. Like two people thinking and feeling the same way about the other, there was no need for any words to be exchanged. They attacked like two pit bulls. Murder caught Rab with a nice combination that put Rab on his ass.

"Naw, muthafucka, get up!" Murder yelled, bouncing around on his toes. "You foul for the way you handled that situation." He wanted nothing more than to stomp Rab's ass.

"Fuck you, nigga! Don't try to put that shit on me," Rab said, jumping to his feet. "You know that's how your bitch ass gets down."

Rab pushed murder and then threw a quick jab, catching Murder by surprise. Before Murder realized it, his ass was in the air.

"Yeah, motherfucker!" Rab yelled, slamming him to the ground.

Rab managed to get some punches in before it turned into a wrestling match.

"Let me up! I'm gonna beat your ass," Murder assured him, preferring to fight on his feet than wrestle on the ground.

"Nigga, fuck you! Why you do Lil' Darryl at his people's

house," Rab asked, struggling to free his hands from Murder's grip so he could throw another punch.

"I didn't do shit! Your bitch ass did," Murder responded, trying to get to his feet.

They went back and forth until they really started to listen to what the other was saying.

"Wait a minute. If you didn't and I didn't, then who the fuck did?" Rab asked as the two men loosened their grip on each other.

*****

Poppa Joe smiled while staring out his bay window. He was undecided if he should expose his hand or keep it hidden. He had everything to gain and nothing to lose. Lil' Darryl was no longer an issue, and the way Sasha's lil' niggas handled their business was amazing. The police didn't know whether to continue questioning the mailman or arrest him for murder. Either way, no one knew the move he had put into play, and by the look of things, it was better off that way.

"What the fuck happened to y'all?" Poppa Joe questioned as Rab and Murder entered his house.

"Just a misunderstanding," Rab responded as he headed towards the kitchen for some ice.

"I don't give a fuck! I want a muthafucka touched in every hood...man, woman or child," Murder barked at his squad.

"Hold up, Murder. What's going on?" Poppa Joe asked.

"Rab nor I put that move on Lil' Darryl, and if a muthafucka thinks it's open season—"

"What the fuck you mean y'all didn't handle it?" Poppa Joe yelled, acting out his role. "If y'all didn't do it, who the fuck did?" he asked, even though he knew they would never be able to answer such a question.

"I don't know, but once I'm finished, a muthafucka is gonna wish they hadn't," Murder assured him, walking to grab himself a drink. "I feel like had I set an example with the Herdo situation, we wouldn't be at this point, a point where a muthafucka thinks it's okay to get at one of us," he added, then threw back his head and downed the drink. "But, don't worry. I'm about to turn up on these niggas."

"You better believe it!" Rab jumped in, holding a bag of ice against his eye.

Despite the fact that innocent people were about to get touched or possibly killed, Poppa Joe held his tongue. He felt this was the way things should have been handled from the start.

"I don't care one way or another. Just handle it."

He loved the way his guys were craving their taste for blood again.

With Herdo's situation and now Lil' Darryl, the wolves within the city began loading their chops, eyeing Poppa Joe and his crew. What was once considered untouchable might as well be touchable.

*****

"I'm telling you, these niggas are so caught up in their own movie that they need to be in Hollywood," Tamisha said, hoping to convince Tone and Freddie to make a play with them. "You already got at Herdo and now somebody touched Lil' Darryl. We might as well take it to the next level and get at Poppa Jo'se ass."

"You're terrible." Tone laughed and shook his head.

"Naw, nigga, I'm an apprentice, and when an opportunity presents itself, I'm not the one to hesitate taking full advantage of it like some niggas I know."

"Calm down, lil' momma," Freddie jumped in. "Just pipe down for a minute. We got some shit in motion. We just politicking if we should bring you on board or not," he added, as if this would be exciting news to Tamisha.

Tamisha looked at Freddie like he was speaking in a

foreign language. She couldn't believe they had the audacity to be thinking about whether or not to include her after all the work she had put in and the plays she had put together.

"When the fuck y'all catch brains and start thinking? Don't do me no favors."

Offended, she stood up and started gathering her things.

"I look better getting up with the nigga that touched Lil' Darryl's ass. The nigga thinks he got the mailman going to jail to serve time for a murder he didn't even commit. Fuck y'all and whatever the hell y'all got going—"

Tone balled up the mailman uniform and threw it at her, smacking her in the face.

"Well, bitch, look no further. You're standing in his presence," he said, taking credit for something his man did.

"Y'all did that?" she asked while looking at the uniform on the floor in disbelief.

"Now sit the fuck down and shut up," Tone barked, hoping she realized now she wasn't dealing with any dummies.

Chapter 12

"That's what the fuck I'm talking about," Murder said, getting the news he wanted to hear from his murder squad. "Y'all lil' niggas fall back until I tell y'all otherwise. I'm gonna shoot Stacks over there to break bread with y'all. Plus, I got a little something extra for you."

He ended the call feeling good that they had handled their business.

Murder got on stage rapping Murking Season by Plies. It caused Angel to ponder what he was insinuating through the lyrics. She hoped like hell Murder hadn't killed a police officer.

"Please, baby, tell me you didn't?"

She knew the murder of a police officer would surely bring her investigation to a close.

"Did what?" he asked, giving her a peck on the lips.

"Don't play with me, Murder." She looked him dead in his eyes.

Murder felt good with the tension in the air. He was lost within his own thoughts, knowing the streets were on fire. Smacking Angel on the ass, he remixed Plies' song "Murkin' Season" while heading upstairs.

"The streets ain't safe. The more rounds you shoot at a nigga, the less aim it takes. It's murkin' season, so you pussy-ass niggas stay out my way."

"Murder, freeze!" she blurted out, then in an attempt to camouflage what she had just said, she quickly added, "Don't you freeze me out."

When Murder turned around, Angel silently prayed she hadn't blown her cover.

"Damn, baby, for a minute I thought you were the police," he said, laughing the situation off while coming back down the stairs.

Blinded by the idea of love and caught up with everything around him, he disregarded one of the basic rules of the streets: Go with your first instinct; it will never mislead you.

"Fuck you, Murder!" Angela said, acting like she was upset about being called the police. "You opened up to me the other day about some serious shit, and now you're around here rapping this murking shit. Let me know what the business is so we can get our alibis straight, because I don't want to lose you."

Putting on an Oscar-winning performance, Angel forced tears to escape her eyes. It was too late in the game to fumble. She was the star quarterback playing in the biggest game of her career.

"Awww, baby." Murder wrapped his arms around her, allowing her to rest her head on his chest. "I'm a lot of things, but I am not a cop killer. I don't need those types of problems in my life right now," he whispered in her ear, causing Angel to smile.

That's all she needed to hear to know her investigation wouldn't be compromised. Still, she was curious to know what murking season was about.

"So what's really going on?" she asked, wiping away her fake tears.

"Some things are better left untold regardless of how bad you want to share things with your better half," he replied, then kissed her on the lips before heading back upstairs.

"You know I love you, right?"

Angel's words caused him to stop in his tracks once

again.

"I love you more," he responded, blowing her a kiss.

As he continued up the stairs, he thought about his next moves.

*****

"What the fuck is going on?" Batman yelled after getting another call from the captain. "How in the hell does four bodies wind up all over the city within six hours? This shit can't be real."

While Batman tried to make sense of it all, Big Country couldn't care less.

"Hell, just let them all kill each other," he suggested.

"I couldn't agree with you more, but with the captain on my ass, I have no choice," Batman said as he sped towards Grant Hospital, hoping to get a statement from somebody.

Ten minutes later, he and Big Country walked right into the midst of a crisis. Mothers stood crying as they faced the reality that their child was no longer amongst the living, while others praised the Lord for allowing theirs to see another day. There were truly mixed emotions amongst the families, but the fact that another black man had lost his life to the streets was heartbreaking to all.

"Lord, why? Why?" one mother cried out, dropping to her knees. "I wasn't supposed to outlive my child, Lord," she sobbed as family and close friends embraced her.

The scene within the waiting room was one many wished they didn't have to endure. Batman surveyed the room, looking for a family he could approach at such a tragic time. The last thing he wanted was to be disrespectful; still, he had a job to do. Before he could choose, one of the male family members approached him.

"Batman, let me speak with you in private," he said.

The two men along with Big Country walked until they were out of earshot of the others. That's when the older gentleman gave Batman an ear full of information, letting him know what the streets were saying and sharing what little information he knew.

"That's crazy he would hurt innocent people behind Lil' Darryl's situation," the older gentleman expressed before returning to console his younger sister, whose son was one of the four people who didn't make it.

After hearing that, nothing else needed to be heard.

"We need to just kill that motherfucker and be done with him," Big Country said as they walked away. He was tired of playing games with Poppa Joe.

Batman, on the other hand, was trying to make sense of it all, but based on the new revelation, his assumptions were obviously wrong.

"His pride is getting the best of him," Batman finally said.

"What does that have to do with anything?" Big Country questioned as they exited the hospital.

"He sees the city slipping through his hands. People are starting to try his ass, and the only way to deal with it is to kill them. But don't worry, partner. This duck is almost ready for plucking," he told Big Country as they jumped into their SUV's.

*****

Despite the streets feeling some type of way, no one dared confront Poppa Joe. He heard the whispers, and as long as they continued to be just that, he didn't give a damn. Poppa Joe treated life like a game of chess; he always made sure he was three moves ahead of his opponent. As he traveled from hood to hood checking the pulse of niggas' hearts, he watched their body language and reactions as he cruised down their blocks. He laughed to himself because he knew they wouldn't try anything with him. It wasn't until he traveled east that he ran into KC at the speedway on Livingston and Brice.

"Fam, what you doing out here like this?" KC asked him, feeling for his steel in the waistband of his pants.

"Nigga, please! I'm good!" Poppa Joe assured him as he got out of his car. "You know I'm on my Gotti shit. Whenever I'm in town, I'm right here in these streets. My jewelry is on, car parked, my shirt off, and no pistol. Ain't not one nigga gonna take nothing," he added, feeling himself. "My lil' niggas always around ready to shake something. These pussies better ask somebody about me, if they don't already know."

"I feel you, but it only takes one of these young, dumb mutherfuckas trying to make a name for themselves. Shit can get ugly really quick."

KC thought about handling Poppa Joe himself and getting it over with. It wasn't that quick to forgive and forget.

"But you know I'll hold you down," he continued, showing Poppa Joe his steel and deciding to let Rab plan out the attack on him like they discussed.

"Why wouldn't you?" Poppa Joe responded arrogantly as if he didn't have a care in the world. "I'm the man in these streets. I'm the one making it happen where muthafuckas will never see a drought again. I'm—"

He continued on and on, putting himself above everyone else. KC half listened, masking his true feelings with a smile so he wouldn't be exposed.

"Alright, fam, I don't mean to run, but I have to handle my business before it gets too late." KC said, turning to walk away.

"How's your hand holding up?" Poppa Joe called out to him, his question taking KC by surprise.

"It's better," he responded, holding up his bandaged hand. "I can't wait until your bitch ass gets everything you have coming to you," KC whispered as he slid behind the steering wheel of his truck.

*****

"I'm telling you, he's wide open, and I love the way y'all handled Lil' Darryl," Sasha said, smiling as they headed towards Franklin Park.

"If that nigga's open, squeeze his ass for more money to handle Batman's ass," Tone suggested as they sped down I-70. "Because I'll handle that nigga; his ass is next," he added.

"No, Tone! No!" Sasha yelled, getting upset. "You always want to take shit too far when it's not even necessary," she added while taking the Board Street exit.

"What the fuck do you mean when it's not necessary? I'll be damned if I allow a nigga, outside of the niggas I rock with, hold some shit like this over my head."

Tone sat straight up in his seat and looked at Sasha. It was a look she hated; he was letting her know she better strap up and get about that life.

They went back and forth until ultimately she sided with him. She began to see things from his point of view versus the way she was looking at things.

"I just hope when this is over, we can live the life I always dreamed of having with you," Sasha said, turning into Franklin Park and searching for a spot to park.

They continued to share their thoughts and dreams with one another, reminiscing about the past and planning for a better future.

Sasha reached over and touched his head as Keyshia Cole's "I Choose You" began to play. When Keyshia started to sing about comparing him to another, Tone got in his feelings.

"How the fuck are you going to compare him to me, Sasha, How?" It was one thing to know she was fucking Poppa Joe, but to know she had genuine feelings for him was more than he could handle.

"I can ask you the same thing, Tone. How can you love her?" she asked, throwing the ball in his court.

Tone turned away. He knew exactly who she was referring to, and despite the fact that he didn't love Tamisha, he was still sleeping with her.

"I don't love her," he finally replied, turning to look Sasha directly in her eyes.

"I hope not, because in this game of love, there are no rules. And when it comes to us, I choose you," Sasha said wholeheartedly as tears escaped her eyes.

"And I choose you," he said.

Kissing her passionately, he hoped to erase any doubt. Tone unbuckled his pants as he tongued her down while Keyshia Cole continued playing in the background.

"I know love is not perfect," she told him, breaking their kiss. "He can give me the world and it will never be enough, because without a doubt, I choose you."

"You talk too much," he said, grabbing the back of her head.

"And you so nasty!" she shot back, not hesitating to give him head like a pornstar right there in the car.

They were so wrapped up in what they were doing that they never noticed the person in the same gray Magnum watching them from afar.

"What the fuck I look like? I'm telling you, I am on his ass, Chin," Tommy C said, keeping Tone in view. "I'm ready to pop his top back."

Tommy C had been following Tone ever since Chin's lawyer informed him to steer clear of everyone connected to Short North, especially until he could get a peek at the names of those who would be indicted. Just the thought of an indictment in Short North sent chills down Chin's spine. Tone was one of his best men, and the secrets they shared between each other could get a nigga a hundred years. So, before he allowed a nigga to bake him a cake, he would crash the birthday party first. Once he and Tommy C blew out the candles, men and women alike would wish they had never been invited.

"Naw, fam, just hold tight. When the time is right, we'll make that move," Chin told him, making his way to see

Layla.

Tommy C became even more frustrated. "Fuck all that. The longer we wait, the greater the risk. Do you want to second-guess your gut instinct when you know this nigga can't hold water?"

He wanted to be proactive and eliminate a problem before it became one.

"I know you don't care too much for dude, but we got history. So, before I bring a play his way, I have to be sure," Chin responded, ending the call. He just hoped he was making the right decision.

Chapter 13

"What's going on in there?" Angel asked as she and Special Agent Johnson walked past the conference room on the way to their office.

"They got this big indictment that's about to come down on the Short North posse and—"

"The Short North what?" Angel said, cutting her partner off.

"The Short North posse, and from what I hear, it's a seventeen-count indictment from drug conspiracy, murder for hire, extortion. You name it, they're charging these guys with it," Special Agent Johnson told her.

"When do they plan on picking up these guys?" she asked out of curiosity.

"That's the crazy part. A lot of them are already locked up doing big numbers," he told her. "They plan on sending them a target letter allowing them an opportunity to tell their story before everything comes crashing down around them," he added, following her into their office.

Knowing how the game was played, Angel laughed.

"So, basically, they're giving them a chance to snitch before the next man."

"Exactly!" he responded, sitting down at his desk.

"Anyway, how are things coming along with the case," Special Agent Johnson inquired as he reclined back in his chair and threw his feet up on the desk.

Angel glanced up from the monthly report she had been looking at. "Believe it or not, it's coming together nicely. Matter of fact, I'll have their asses bagged and tagged before the end of summer," she replied with confidence.

Her partner chuckled. "Yeah, right. You're so cocky. Would you be interested in putting something on the line?" he asked, hoping she would jump out there.

Angel turned her attention from her computer and looked at him. "Why wouldn't I be? I'm never scared." Seeing the mischievous look plastered all over his face, she told him, "And while you're sitting there smiling, make it lighter on yourself."

She knew he had something up his sleeve.

"Let's just say when I win, it will not cost you anything out of pocket, but it will cost you."

He stood up to reposition the erection in his pants, letting her know exactly what was on his mind. Angela shook her head, indicating she was aware of what he was insinuating.

"Are you sure that's what you want? Because if I win, I got this strap-on I've been anxious to use on a motherfucker." She let him know two could play that game.

"Picture that!" he said, looking at her like she was crazy.

"Yeah, picture that," she shot back, smiling.

*****

"Damn, bitch, where you at?" Layla asked. She had just ordered a shot of 1738.

"Breaking every law trying to get to your crazy ass," Sasha replied playfully as she sped down the highway.

"I hope so. The last thing I need is for these Chinese

motherfuckers to think I'm here by myself." Layla laughed before taking a shot to the head.

"And why is that?" Sasha asked, entertaining her girl's conversation.

"They will have a bitch drugged up, dragged to the back, and on the menu within the hour. By the time you get here, they'll be trying to serve me as their special for today."

Layla started laughing so hard that she almost spilled the second drink she had ordered.

"Girl, bye!" Sasha hung up on her girl but couldn't help laughing herself.

Layla sat in Genju's Chinese Restaurant with a hell of a dilemma on her hands as she waited for the two most important people in her life to arrive. She hated Tone for being the riff between her girls. If only he had kept his dick to himself. Tone wasn't the only one to blame, though. Despite her hoeish ways, Tamisha knew better than to fuck her girl's man.

As Layla pondered the situation, Tamisha walked through the door.

"Hey, girl," Tamisha said, greeting Layla with a hug.

"Look at you," Layla replied, observing her from head to toe.

"I see I'm not the only one getting at the money," Tamisha told her girl while taking a seat next to her girl.

"I wish I could take the credit, but if it wasn't for Sasha breaking bread from afar, I'd still be on the back page," Layla responded, laughing at her statement.

The mention of Sasha's name caused Tamisha to squirm in her seat.

"Fuck that bitch. I got you if you need anything," Tamisha said, then reached in her purse and pulled out a bankroll of money.

"I see scratching up your knees is really paying off for

you." The sound of Sasha's voice caused the two women to turn in their chairs.

At that moment, the tension in the air became thick as Tamisha and Sasha stared at each another. It was like an imaginary line had been drawn. Even though Tamisha had committed an act of betrayal, Sasha had no desire to beat her ass over no dick, only if Tamisha crossed the line and played her close.

"I wouldn't know," Tamisha responded, blowing off Sasha's comment as she turned back around.

"That's what your mouth says," Sasha said, trying to provoke her.

"Come on now, y'all," Layla jumped in, feeling caught in the middle.

"What? You thought this was going to be a happy reunion?" Sasha took a seat on the other side of Layla.

Tamisha just laughed as she paid for the drink she had ordered. "Bitch, don't get mad 'cause your sweet lil' Tone jumped the fence for greener pastures," she said, putting it all out there to stop the speculations.

"Believe me, I'm not." Sasha seemed unfazed by Tamisha's attempt to jab at her. "You think you doing something? That nigga is in more bitches' beds than bed bugs. You're a stupid-ass bitch."

Sasha laughed like she had the upper hand.

Layla sat there and let them go back and forth until she felt like it was enough.

"That's it!" she yelled, throwing her hands in the air. "I've heard enough of the bullshit." She looked at both the girls. "I didn't call y'all here for this. We've been girls for way too long to let anything come between us, especially some dick. I don't care if his dick is made of gold. We'll trick his ass out before anything else," Layla said, trying to make light of the situation.

She went on to tell her girls to learn from the past and

move forward.

"In our lives, we will endure pain, but it will strengthen our bond. I said all that to say this: Together we stand; divided we fall; and any motherfucker that tries to come between us, may he rest in peace."

With those words, Layla let it be known what it was.

Sasha left the restaurant with mixed emotions. Yes, she agreed with most of what Layla had said, but she still found it hard to get over Tamisha's betrayal. It wasn't about her fucking Tone, because the nigga would fuck a snake if you held its mouth open long enough. The thing that bothered Sasha the most was Tamisha's lack of remorse.

Had it been me who fucked one of her niggas, a bitch would've been trying to fight, she thought as she walked in the house.

Sasha had a lot on her mind, and Tamisha fucking her man was the least of them. She had a plan to get money and get out of dodge with Tone. Unfortunately, a few lives would be lost in the process, including those she didn't intend to hurt.

*****

"Damn, Poppa Joe, I wish I could."

"You wish you could what?" Poppa Joe surprised her standing by the driver's side door.

He had seen her pull into the driveway. When she didn't exit the vehicle right away, he took it upon himself to see what was up.

Startled, Sasha grabbed her heart. She didn't know how she allowed him to sneak up on her.

"Boy, don't make me fuck you up! How long you've been standing there?" she asked, gathering her things as he opened the door for her.

"Not that long. Seems like you were in a daze when you whispered something about wishing you could..." Poppa

Joe's voice trailed off as he waited for her explain.

"It's just so crazy," Sasha said, thinking quickly. "I just came from seeing my girls, and they're feeling some type of way because I don't come around as much now that I'm with you. I wish I could make everyone happy without disappointing the other."

She looked up at him, hoping he would believe her and offer some type of advice.

"What do they want you to do? Call more, come around more, or leave me?" Poppa Joe responded. The thought of her leaving pained him.

"No, bae, it ain't nothing like that. They know you make me happy, and so they are happy for me."

"Well, as long as it's not the latter of the three, you'll figure it out," he said and kissed her on the lips, relieved that her girls weren't trying to get her to leave him.

As Sasha walked toward the house, she gave herself a pat on the back for being able to dodge a bullet and not reveal what she really wished she could do versus the excuse she gave him.

"Hey, Murder," she said, entering the house. "Where's my girl?"

She stopped for a moment to put her phone on the charger.

"She's upstairs somewhere," he replied while channel surfing.

Shaking her head, she proceeded to walk up the steps in search of Angel. Once she reached the top of the stairs, she felt the urge to use the bathroom. When she walked in, she couldn't believe what she saw.

"Bitch, what the fuck is that?" she yelled, looking at Angel.

Angel froze, not knowing how to respond. Then she quickly pulled Sasha into the bathroom and closed the door.

"Bitch, lower your fucking voice."

Wasn't any sense in trying to cover up what had already

been exposed. Angel was in the bathroom adjusting the wire she had on when Sasha unexpectedly entered.

"You the police?" Sasha asked, her eyes wide. She suddenly wondered how she was going to make her move and put distance between her and her life.

"Sasha, you're not who I'm after, and whatever you and your boyfriend got going on, ain't none of my business as long as it doesn't interfere with my shit," Angel told her, letting Sasha know she knew more than she realized.

"My boyfriend's downstairs, and it looks like you're already at his head. So, miss me with that bullshit you spitting."

Ready to go tell Poppa Joe, Sasha started walking toward the door.

Angel moved out the way as Sasha got closer, but just when she grabbed the doorknob to leave, Angel told her, "Bad boys ain't no good; good boys ain't no fun. Lord knows you better run off with the right one."

Angel then moved toward the mirror so she could get back to her business of concealing the wire. "That's the boyfriend I'm talking about, not the one you're playing house with."

Smiling at Sasha through the reflection in the mirror, Angel knew what she had just revealed would stop Sasha dead in her tracks.

True enough, Sasha stood frozen in the doorway wondering how she knew about Tone.

"Don't look surprised. I've been on to you ever since I heard y'all conversation at the Moonlight." Angel turned and took a couple steps toward Sasha. "And I must say he's a cutie. But like I said, don't bring whatever you're cooking back to my table of investigations."

She paused while standing directly in front of Sasha.

"If you can do that, then we good," she finished, blowing Sasha a kiss as she walked away.

Sasha looked on as Angel sashayed down the steps,

wondering what she had gotten herself into.

*****

On the other side of town, Tone voiced the same thing Sasha was thinking.

"What the fuck have I gotten myself into?" he said, while reading a letter from his mother called him over to read.

"What do it say?" Freddie asked, concerned with the expression on his man's face.

Tone looked at Freddie as he tried to make sense of it all.

"The Feds want me to come down to the federal building and holler at them," Tone finally said.

"Holler at them about what?" Freddie snapped. "We don't speak Pig Latin," he added, waiting on Tone to agree.

"That goes without saying. Fuck them bitches," he replied, balling up the letter to get his point across and save face in front of his man.

Several days later, Tone did the unthinkable and made a trip to the federal building unknowingly to anyone. After countless hours of talking, it didn't take a rocket scientist to figure out they already had him bagged and tagged.

"If y'all have all this on me, why the fuck am I not in handcuffs?" Tone yelled, looking around at the agents.

He sat there madder than a motherfucker, mostly at himself. He knew the catching comes before the hanging, and for him, he had to be the stupidest person walking the planet.

"Calm down, Mr. Jones. There's a reason for everything. True enough, we got you locked in on this murder hands down. But, if you help us, I promise you will see the light of day once these indictments come down," the agent explained.

Tone sat there as they revealed the people involved. He became lost in thought while looking at the pictures of those people taped on a dry erase board. Shit was actually real and not a nightmare.

"We have all the pieces to the puzzle. We're just giving

you the opportunity to help us put the next man in line for the same opportunity. The choice is yours," the agent finished.

Over the years, the agent had grown tired of trying to save young black men who didn't want to save themselves.

While looking at the pictures on the board, Tone weighed his options. A few of them he considered to be friends; a lot of them he didn't know or just didn't care about them. Then an image of Sasha flashed within his mind and everything else became a no-brainer.

"What do y'all want to know?" he said as a single tear rolled down his cheek.

In that instant, he became something he never envisioned he would ever become.

Chapter 14

"Come on, Rab. Hear me out. I know that's your man, but he ain't good for the team. He's a liability and he talks too fuckin' much. That shit is only going to cause problems in the long run," Batman said, letting him know KC had to go.

"I don't know," Rab responded, not wanting to betray his man. "I got love for that nigga, but if it's true what you're saying, I might have no choice."

Rab turned and went to go look out the window. He needed to gather his thoughts.

Seeing that Rab was still undecided, Batman tried to decide if he should put the icing on the cake. If he didn't know anything else, he knew money would turn the best of friends against each other.

"Everything happens for a reason," he said, pressing for Rab to decide.

"How is that, Batman? Tell me how is that?" Rab wasn't feeling the whole conversation of killing his man.

"No matter how you want to look at it, your boy has to go. So why not get paid doing that?" Batman said, throwing his bait out there.

The mention of money sparked Rab's interest.

"How so?" he asked, turning to give Batman his full attention.

Batman smiled. He loved his ability to play off one's

greed.

"My boy Big Country and I are going to run up in Poppa Joe's spot and not only handle KC, but rob the spot, too. How much we all walk away with depends on when we do it."

He looked at Rab to see if understood what he was saying.

"Now you talking my lingo," Rab said, causing both men to laugh.

Rab started to see all the free money he could easily walk away with and not even get his hands dirty. Now the thought of killing KC didn't seem that bad after all, especially when he stood to gain a small fortune. His next question didn't surprise Batman at all. He knew money was the root of every man's greed and could cloud a person's judgement, resulting in them doing things they normally wouldn't do.

"So what will be my take?" Rab asked and then waited for the million-dollar response.

"Bands, babbbby," Batman yelled, smiling as he rubbed his hands together.

*****

"Nigga, what's wrong with you?" Freddie asked, looking at his man sideways. "You been on some funny shit lately."

"Naw, I just been thinking about getting at Batman and getting that money. Once we hit that lick, I'm getting the fuck out of Columbus," Tone told him, meaning every word.

Tone was at a crossroad in his life. He didn't know if he should expose his hand or keep quiet and allow his man to continue walking on the blind side.

"Nigga, where are you going to go? Columbus is all we know. Plus, once we hit this lick, we'll be in position to take over this muthafucka," Freddie said, giving his point of view.

Tone shook his head as if he agreed, but honestly, he was only trying to disguise his betrayal. He loved his man, but he loved himself and his freedom a whole lot more.

"You're right. Where the fuck am I going to go? Once

this lick goes down, Columbus is ours," he concurred, telling Freddie what he wanted to hear.

"That's what the fuck I'm talking about! You had me worried for a minute." Freddie dapped up his man. "I'm on my way to meet Misha. She claims she got a nigga rapping, you know what I'm talking about," he added, smiling from ear to ear because he knew that meant there was money to be made.

"You go do that. Tell her to holla at your boy. I'm going to holla at ole boy to hit that lick on Batman's ass," Tone said, turning on his heels.

He was more determined than ever to hit that lick and get the hell out of Columbus. Cincinnati is where he would be headed; he had a couple cousins down that way. Tone needed to put as much distance between him and Columbus before those indictments touched down. The last thing he wanted to do was own up to what he had done and have to see the look on his guy's face. The guys who he grew up with, skipped school with, and bodied niggas with would be going to jail for the same shit he was down with.

"Fuck them niggas!" he reasoned with himself as he jumped into his SUV. "Once I set this bitch up in flames, they're going to know what it is. Columbus on fire, muthafucka!"

*****

After talking to Sasha, Tone wasn't too sure if she had what it took to see things through. The whole time while he was talking with her about how he planned to make things happen, she stared off into space. It was as if she had something to say but chose not say it. So, instead of trying to press her or risk her changing her mind, Tone opted to leave well enough alone and focus on what he needed to do.

For the next few weeks, Tone and Freddie stalked Batman, hoping to catch him slipping in order to use a plan from their playbook.

"Nigga, you tripping," Freddie said as they drove through the city in search of Batman. "I say we set it off on sight. We have the element surprise to our advantage, and the muthafucka will never see it coming," he added, thinking he had the perfect plan.

"Nigga, you're crazier than I thought, if you think I'm putting my freedom at risk for some bullshit plan like that," Tone responded, shaking his head.

"Fuck you!" Freddie replied, not knowing what else to say. "Don't worry, my nigga, once I catch this muthafucka slipping to where I can put this on his shit, we're gonna be able to fuck him off at any given time. You feel me?" Freddie smiled at his man as they headed up north.

"Nigga, you sound serious about this shit," Tone said, liking his man's idea better than his own.

"Why wouldn't I be? Especially with a half a million at stake," Freddie said with a grin.

*****

"I'm still charging niggas like I'm supposed to, still testing niggas like I'm supposed to. You muthafuckas keep watching me like you supposed to, because I'ma keep grinding like I'm supposed to," Tamisha rapped, feeling herself as she remixed Gucci Mane's lyrics.

"Bitch, you too much," Layla said, seeing a totally different side to her girl.

She knew Tamisha was special, but didn't know to what extent until she heard her spit her own remix. The part about scheming and setting niggas up shed light on what she was actually doing with Tone and Freddie.

"Bitch, I hope you're not into what I think you're into, because Tone and Freddie will have your ass in a world of trouble you won't be able to get out of," Layla told her, hoping Tamisha wasn't that foolish to let them drop her off.

"You worry about the wrong things. You need to worry about what the hell I got them into, because at the end of the day, I'm getting money like I'm supposed to." She blew Layla a kiss and disappeared down the hallway.

Layla shook her head, not knowing how to take what she'd just shared.

"I just hope you be careful like you supposed to," Layla whispered to herself, hoping Tamisha wasn't getting in too deep. "Yeah, girl, just be careful.

*****

In the middle of the night, Tone exited his spot with his laptop in hand. After quickly jumping into his car, he set up the laptop on the passenger seat and smiled as he powered it on. It had been three days since he placed the tracking device under Batman's truck, and three consecutive nights Batman's truck had been parked in the same location. Tone believed it was where Batman laid his head, the perfect spot to catch him slipping.

"I hope you got room for a nigga at the breakfast table," he said, laughing as he pulled off and followed the directions on his laptop to Batman's location.

Twenty minutes later, Tone pulled into a condo complex up north. He drove straight to where Batman had his truck parked.

"There it is," he said, then looked for the perfect spot to park so he could observe his surroundings.

While he sat ducked off waiting on Batman to appear, he sparked a blunt and texted back and forth with a female he met until early in the morning. That's when he spotted Batman exiting one of the condos. He got so excited that he dropped his phone between the seats.

"I know where you lay your head at," he sang, but what he saw next caused his mouth to drop. "What the fuck?"

He almost threw up at the sight before him. He wanted to

jump out his car and kill both of them.

"How the fuck did this shit happen?"

He watched his cousin Tasha B and Batman trade kisses. After allowing Batman to pull off, Tone sat there in deep thought before he pulled off, as well. Driving back to his spot, he still couldn't come to grips with what he had just witnessed.

"This can't be," he said to himself, bumping into Freddie entering the spot.

"What's that?" Freddie responded, seeing the puzzled look on his man's face.

"Tasha," Tone replied as he walked straight into the living room and took a seat.

"Your cousin Tasha B?" Freddie asked, following right behind him.

"Yes." Tone covered his face with the palm of his hands.

"What about her?" Freddie inquired, wondering what she could have possibly done to have him like this.

"She's fucking Batman!" Tone blurted.

"Get the fuck outta here!" He couldn't believe what he heard. "Not crazy, loud-mouth Tasha B," he added, trying to make sure they were talking about the same person.

"The one and only, and to top it off, the bitch is pregnant," Tone said, revealing the most hurtful part of all…that his cousin was sleeping with the enemy.

For the next few minutes, time seemed to stand still as Tone pictured his cousin not only fucking with the enemy but bringing his offspring into the world, as well.

"Not in this lifetime," Tone said, breaking the silence between them. "Shit, I guess it is what it is. She made her choice," he added, standing up and looking at Freddie. "And for a half a mill, she can get it, too."

He had made up his mind that nothing would stand in the way of him getting his money, not even flesh and blood!

"That's what I'm talking about," Freddie said, glad that his man didn't have a change of heart. "So when do we make our move?"

"No sooner than the money is in place and not a second later," Tone responded, then left the room.

*****

"Poppa Joe!" Stacks yelled. Walking into the house, he caught a glimpse of Angel wearing a two-piece bikini. "Girl, you lucky you fuck with my man, because I'll have you—"

"You'll have her what?" Poppa Joe said, cutting Stacks off as he entered the room.

"I'll have her ass looking for a nigga in broad daylight with a flashlight," he responded, not backing down from what he was about to say.

"Yeah, right," Angel said, blowing him off. "You couldn't stand the pressure with a bitch like me. I'll have your young ass sprung, dumb, and walking into the bank with a note."

They all were laughing at her comment when Murder entered the room.

"What's funny?" Murder asked.

"Stacks is ready to rob a bank," Angel told him know, causing Poppa Joe and Stacks to laugh even more.

Not knowing what the hell was going on, Murder decided to just join them in laughing.

"Anyway, shit's all ready to go and ole boy said everything is everything," Stacks informed Poppa Joe, causing him to shake his head.

"That's what's up," Poppa Joe replied.

He knew exactly what Stacks was talking about, and he couldn't wait to make this move. Poppa Joe had taken a hell of a lost surrounding Shamar's gay ass, after that lost, he had to think fast and move just as fast to come up with the money he was short paying his connect.

"You know Bay Bay and them been hitting my sack like crazy," Murder said, talking about the plug in Miami.

"I already know, but once I make this move with Primo and them out west, I'll be getting at them ASAP." Poppa Joe knew he couldn't prolong getting at his plug much longer.

Angel stood there taking everything in. She understood what was being said without it actually being said. She smiled, putting together what many would never have guessed. Despite the front Poppa Joe put on, he was fucked up after having taken that loss at his stash spot. He needed to make a move in the city in order to make things right with his plug.

"Un-fucking-believable," she whispered to herself, seeing things for what they really were and not what Poppa Joe wanted everyone to believe.

Chapter 15

A few weeks later, Poppa Joe had made things right with his plug and was sitting on top of the world again. With his birthday only a few days away, he planned on making it an event that many would never forget.

"You see this?" Batman yelled, slamming some papers on his desk. "This motherfucker got a permit to throw a birthday bash in my city…and out of all places, Franklin Park."

He turned redder than a stop sign.

"Calm down, partner," Big Country responded. "There's nothing we can do about it now, especially with him having a permit. Let's just make it a birthday he'll never forget."

As he listened to his partner, Batman began to calm down while envisioning the kind of gift he wanted to surprise Poppa Joe with on his birthday.

"Yeah, Big Country, we're gonna give him something he'll never see coming," Batman said with a smile that meant there would be trouble for Poppa Joe.

For the rest of the day, Batman went about his business of extorting the city's mid-level drug dealers and lining up his play for Poppa Joe's birthday party.

"I'm telling you, Rab, it will be the perfect day. Won't nobody be expecting it, you feel me?" Batman said, putting Rab down with the move.

Rab acted like he was undecided, but secretly, he was ready to make it happen.

"I don't know, Batman. If you say so. I can't do nothing but trust you and allow things to fall into place. What I want more than anything, though, is to dead Poppa Joe's bitch ass so I can start running this shit."

He wanted him out the way bad.

"Don't worry, Rab, everything's gonna fall into place. Just be patient. I got you," Batman assured him.

They had to be smart, because sometimes when playing with fire, you're the one who ends up getting burned in the end. Rab could not make the mistake of being blinded by his greed for wanting to be the head nigga in charge. No matter how carefully you love, treat, or handle a snake, it will always be one!

Despite the bad blood many felt toward Poppa Joe and his crew, the city was buzzing like crazy about his birthday bash in Franklin Park. The love for free food, drinks, and live entertainment was enough to reconcile any differences.

"The city is gonna love me after this one." Poppa Joe stated as he threw two-hundred-thousand-dollars' worth of dollar bills in a trash bag. "I'ma make it rain on these niggas."

He laughed while envisioning how things would play out.

*****

Franklin Park was packed to capacity, and law enforcement was intent on shutting things down.

"Naw, y'all, don't even think about it," Batman said, surprising everyone. "Let him have his day, 'cause believe me, I'm gonna have mine."

As a helicopter came into view, many believed it was Channel 6 News covering the event. However, they were soon proven wrong when money began to pour out the windows. There was no question about who was in the helicopter then.

"Poppa Joe! Poppa Joe!" the crowd chanted as he made it rain.

In his feelings, Batman shook his head and looked on as money flowed down from the skies. Then the sound of four-wheelers stormed the park out of nowhere, one hundred deep. One after another, they stormed the field, causing the crowd to part and allow them to ride around in one big circle making room for the helicopter to land.

"Un-fucking-believable," Big Country said, witnessing how masterfully everything came together.

Batman looked over at his partner. "If you're so in awe, drop to your knees and blow the muthafuckin' candle. Just run over there and see what the fuck is going on."

Following orders, Big Country stormed off.

Poppa Joe sat in the helicopter with Sasha by his side and Murder, Angel, and Cruzzi seated across from him. As the helicopter began to land, he looked out the window at his guys acting a fool on their four-wheelers. He knew his grand entrance would be the talk of the city for years to come.

"You didn't have to do them like this," Murder said as he watched the few bills still swirling in the air.

"How else could I have done it?" Poppa Joe responded, throwing the question right back at his man.

The whole atmosphere was something straight out the scene of a movie.

"Let's get it!" Poppa Joe said, leading the way.

Once the crowd saw him exit the helicopter, they began chanting his name again. Before Batman could make his presence known, Poppa Joe had disappeared within the crowd and was headed towards the stage. Once everyone was in place, Stacks took to the stage and blessed the crowd with a few of his local hits until it was time for Cruzzi to hit the stage.

"Fuck that nigga," Tone said, walking through the maze of people in Franklin Park. "I can't wait until his ass puts that money in place instead of throwing it out a fucking helicopter."

He wasn't impressed with the grand entrance.

"I definitely feel you on that, but best believe his bitch ass is gonna get at us. Because one thing for certain and two things for sure, them faggot-ass niggas on his team ain't about that life," Freddie said, meaning every word as they stood off to the side listening to Cruzzi performing.

"You ain't never lied," Tone responded, rocking to the music. "Matter of fact, this ain't no life you can tag in and out of. Either you in or you ain't; there's no in-between with this shit," he added, feeling himself.

Tone had it all figured out. Or at least that's what he believed since he had the benefit of knowing what was going to happen before it actually did.

"What the fuck got you cheesing?" Freddie asked, looking at the smirk on his man's face.

"It ain't nothing, my nigga. Stop faking and get about this life. You feel me?"

Tone gave his man only the half-truth about the situation versus the whole truth that would reveal his betrayal.

"Now that's something to smile about," Freddie replied, unaware that his freedom was on borrowed time.

Cruzzi rocked the stage but couldn't keep his eyes off Tamisha and Layla. Both women were enticing, and he didn't know which one to choose. So, instead of selling himself short, he opted to try his hand with both of them.

"Why your boy keep eye fucking a bitch?" Layla asked her girl, while rocking to his music. "He must don't know."

"Know what?" Sasha asked, turning to her girl while continuing to do her one-two step.

"That I will fuck him, love him, and leave him heartbroken." Layla laughed like she had said something amazing.

Tamisha heard her girl talking and jumped in the conversation.

"He'd look better fucking with you, because I'll have his ass not able to move or talk; the doctors thinking he might not be able to walk; one bullet in the head and five in his heart,"

Tamisha rapped, holding her fingers in the shape of a gun and pointing them in Cruzzi's direction.

Cruzzi peeped shorty's gesture, and feeling some type of way, he made it known to her how he felt when he hit his last song for the night.

"Eighty chains going and ain't a nigga took one yet; ain't nothing retarded about me but this gold Rolex. Ten thousand bounty put on my neck, hope you didn't pay them cause they didn't have no success." Directing his lyrics straight at Tamisha.

"Girl, see what you done started!" Layla said, turning to her girl.

"Bitch, please. That's foreplay, because he definitely can get it." Tamisha blew him a kiss, letting the games begin.

Layla became so upset that Sasha had to settle her down.

"There's no understanding when the shit on—"

"Don't even say it," Sasha said, cutting her off.

"God, please bless this poor child for she knows not what she's doing." Layla said while holding her hand over her heart and looking to the Lord above.

"Amen," Sasha and Layla said in unison as they looked at Tamisha.

*****

Batman circled the park smiling like it was his birthday. He knew Poppa Joe would surely burst a blood vessel once he touched him where it would hurt the most...his pockets.

"Big Country, where you at?" he said over his two-way.

"I'm on my way to the parking lot," Big Country replied, eyeing some females he would've loved to have his way with.

"Make sure you have the guys ready, because it's going down tonight," Batman said as he made his way to the parking lot.

"No doubt," Big Country responded, jumping into his SUV.

The two men continued conversing until Batman made it to his SUV, which was parked right next to his partner's.

"You know what the word is around the park?" Big Country paused to make sure he had Batman's attention. "The motherfucker dumped a half a mill onto the crowd."

"Get the fuck out of here!" Batman snapped. "You know what? It don't even matter, because if he did, he's going to wish he hadn't after tonight."

Batman considered what he stood to gain and not what Poppa Joe foolishly threw his way.

As he drove off, he went over everything in his mind. The thought of sticking it to Poppa Joe once again caused him to get an erection.

"Damn, Lil' Batman, I didn't know you could grow like that." He looked down, feeling like he had the biggest dick in the world. "I'm far from gay, but I'm going to enjoy fucking you."

He laughed as he hit the highway with nothing on his mind but Poppa Joe.

*****

As the birthday bash at Franklin Park came to an end, people started pairing up with the ones they choose to go fuck for the night and others they promised to meet up with later. Either way it was going down.

"Y'all ready?" Poppa Joe asked, ready to make his exit.

"You already know," Murder responded, grabbing Angel's hand.

"Y'all go ahead. I see someone I'm going to ride...I mean, get a ride with," Cruzzi claimed, looking at Tamisha.

"Good choice," Tamisha said, making her way toward him.

Poppa Joe looked at the two of them and shook his head. "Well, dig, y'all take the chopper. The crew and I will just hightail it out of here on these four-wheelers."

He wasn't about to let Cruzzi wander into the crowd and have to deal with one of those fools trying to make a name for themselves.

Without another word being spoken, Cruzzi and Tamisha took off in the helicopter. Everyone else jumped on the four-wheelers, leaving KC and Rab with Tamisha's car.

"Man, that's some gay-ass shit that nigga just did," KC stated as he and Rab stood there looking stupid. "I can't wait until we handle that situation. I swear I can't wait."

"Don't even trip, nigga. Shit is about to come full circle," Rab told him while watching Poppa Joe and the others ride off. "Trust me, their time on top is only temporary."

Chapter 16

After meeting up with the crew and partying into the wee hours of the morning, KC grabbed him a little cutie and headed home.

"What are you going to do with all this?" the tipsy female asked, turning around so she could feel KC's dick pressed against her ass.

"What do you think I'm gonna do with it?" he said, closing the door behind him.

It was a little past three o'clock in the morning, and KC wasn't in the mood for a whole lot of talking. He was trying to fuck.

"Shhhh!" he said, quickly pushing down on her. "Come here. The police are coming, and I need you to hide this," he told her, pulling out his dick.

"Boy, look at you." The female looked at KC, who exposed himself, and then asked what had to be one of the dumbest questions he'd ever heard. "Where do you want me to hide it?"

"Bitch, don't play dumb. I'm sure you'll find somewhere to hide this motherfucker, whether it's your mouth, pussy, or eye," he responded, stroking himself while he waited for her to choose.

"My eye?" Looking at him sideways, she laughed.

"Yeah, bitch. Not the one that winks; the one that stinks," he said, making his way to her.

Within seconds, KC had shorty on her knees and was making the decision for her.

"That's right, baby. Hide this dick for daddy."

He slowly moved in and out of her mouth until they caught the rhythm. Ms. Lady got to hiding the dick so good that he had to snatch it out her mouth before he exploded.

"Damn, girl, your head game is official," he complimented as he helped pull her up from her knees. "Let's see how good that pussy is."

KC turned her around, hiked up her dress, and bent her over the couch. Then he slid right in and began having his way with her...smacking her ass, pulling her hair, and doing everything else he could think of.

"That's right, baby. Hide this dick. Hide this motherfucker." He paused long enough to step out of his pants and then returned to slamming in and out of her pussy. "Hold up. Take this shit off," he demanded, totally undressing her before laying her on the couch.

They were going at it like wild animals in heat.

"Give me that dick. Don't hold it back."

She met him thrust for thrust. Not to be outdone, KC pushed her legs back to her ears and masterfully pounded her pussy. Then he pushed the limit and slid inside her asshole.

"That's right! Take all of me." Her screams took KC by surprise, sending him over the edge.

"You're gonna catch this muthafuckin' nut," he told her, trying to see just how far she would let him go.

"You ain't said nothing, nigga."

On the verge of cumming, KC pulled his dick out of her ass and allowed her to suck the nut that erupted from his dick.

"Oh yes," he panted as she swallowed ever drop.

After forty-five minutes of straight sucking and fucking,

everything came to an end. That's when they heard the sound of clapping. Startled, they both jumped.

"What the fuck?" KC said, looking up to see Batman and his crew appear from out of the shadows.

They had been in KC's spot the whole time waiting on him to arrive. Once he came through the door and went straight to getting busy with his company, they backed off.

"Calm down, playboy. We were nice enough to let you finish," Batman said, coming into view with his gun pointed at KC.

The female was terrified at first, not knowing who the men were until she heard Batman's name. Then she became embarrassed by the fact that the police had watched as she did freaky things to someone she hardly knew.

"And I must say, Ms. Lady, you know how to hide things well," Batman commented, causing his crew to laugh.

"What's going on, Batman? I know you fuck with my guy. So what's all this about?" KC asked while standing butt-naked with his dick hanging.

"You're right, KC. I do fuck with your guy, but your guy doesn't fuck with you."

Batman's words shocked KC.

"Stop playing. My people and I was just kicking it a few hours ago." KC knew there had to be some misunderstanding.

"I'm not saying you wasn't, and honestly, KC, I don't give a fuc," Batman said before ending KC and the young lady's life with double shots to the head.

"What's wrong with you?" Batman asked when he saw Big Country shaking his head.

"That was some good pussy gone to waste," he replied, wishing he'd gotten the opportunity to have her hide his dick.

"You didn't want that bitch after that nigga had her. He had herpes. A muthafucka should've been killed his ass for spreading that shit throughout the city." Batman grabbed the

141

cans of gasoline and started pouring the flammable liquid over KC and the young lady. "We got everything we came here for. Let's load up the trucks and get out of here."

They made sure they poured the rest of the gasoline throughout the house.

"Don't worry, KC. Your guy is next," Batman whispered before lighting a match and setting the place on fire.

As Batman stood watching the flames grow, he felt powerful. At times, he compared himself to God, deciding who lived and who died.

"See your bitch ass in hell," he said with a laugh before walking out the door. "Columbus on fire, muthafucka."

*****

"You mean to tell me what!" Poppa Joe yelled into the phone. His blood pressure shot to the moon. "Do you have any clue what the fuck I just lost behind this shit?"

Poppa Joe threw his phone across the room before the person had a chance to answer. He couldn't stand to hear another word. The thought of falling that far in the hole to his connect was unthinkable, especially after just making things right a few weeks ago.

"I can't believe this shit," he mumbled, thinking about the five million KC owed.

Several minutes later, Murder, Rab, and Stacks found themselves once again sitting at the round table while waiting for Poppa Joe to enter. With this type of money missing, everybody was suspect. Five million wasn't chump change.

When Poppa Joe entered the room, he looked at the three people sitting before him. He could feel his chest tightening as he began to sweat. He tried to keep his cool, though.

"I know by now somebody got something to tell me. Don't just sit there looking like The Three Stooges," he said, wiping the sweat from his forehead with his hand.

Murder sat there looking at him, knowing something wasn't right.

"You alright, fam? You don't look too good," Murder asked, truly concerned about his man.

Poppa Joe didn't hesitate to respond. "What the fuck—"

Before he could say anything more, he fell to the floor holding his chest.

"Pop!" Stacks and Murder yelled, rushing to his aid.

"Call 911!" Stacks yelled at Rab, who was just standing there watching.

When Murder looked back at him, he could have sworn he saw Rab smirking. With everything going on, he couldn't address it at the moment. He was more concerned about Poppa Joe's well-being than anything else.

*****

"This is what the fuck I'm talking about," Batman yelled, looking at two hundred kilos of cocaine. "We hit the motherload with this one."

He knew Poppa Joe would have a fit.

"Happy birthday, muthafucka!" he shouted, causing his crew to bust out laughing.

"Hell yeah," Big Country jumped in. In his mind, he tried to calculate how much money they were going to make.

"I told y'all this is only the beginning. If y'all rock with me, I'll make all of us millions," Batman said, then paused to allow time for his words to sink in. "The hardest part is over. Now it's time to grind. We're going to flood the streets with this shit, but we can't be foolish by drawing attention to ourselves with excessive spending. If y'all listen and follow my lead, I promise you the best is yet to come."

*****

News of Poppa Joe's hospitalization traveled throughout the city like lightening. Everyone believed all the partying and drinking had caught up to him, but many within his inner circle knew differently. The thought of being five million in the hole to anybody would cause a nigga to have a heart attack.

"I swear that nigga Rab had a smirk on his face," Murder told Stacks as they exited the hospital.

"To tell you the truth, I never trusted him," Stacks responded, ready to reveal something he had noticed a while back but never mentioned. "Remember when shit went down with Sharma? I'm telling you, that nigga was still rocking long after we ran out."

"Get the fuck out of here! Seriously? 'Cause at first, I thought one of my plays was bullshitting when they told me that they copped from the nigga. I pushed down on his ass like, 'What's up,' and the nigga hit me with, 'Oh, that's some snorer's dreams and water nightmare shit," Murder told him, recalling the conversation word for word.

"Well, dig, we're gonna pull the rug from underneath his ass and see if the nigga's still standing. "Then after that…" Stacks voice trailed off as he looked back at the hospital, hoping his man would make a fast recovery.

*****

"I got here as soon as I heard." Layla rushed in the hospital room and over to Sasha, trying to comfort her.

Sasha was an emotional wreck. She fought with herself about if she was betraying Tone for the way she felt about Poppa Joe.

"Thanks, girl," Sasha said, embracing.

No matter what she had been planning, it didn't even matter. She stood by Poppa Joe's side like a down-ass chick was supposed to and when a nigga needed her the most.

"The doctors say he good. He just needed to rest and stop stressing so much," Sasha told Layla as she took a seat in the chair next to Poppa Joe's bed.

"That's easy for them to say. They can't imagine what a nigga like him goes through on a daily basis," Layla expressed.

Poppa Joe lay there with his eyes closed, listening as they freely talked about him and everything else going on. He listened to Layla question her but was surprised when Sasha claimed to know nothing.

"I just hope he pulls through and stop taking life for granted. There is so much more to life than having to keep looking over your shoulder watching these niggas, bitches, and the fucking police. It's all too much, and nine out of ten, it's always the ones you least expect who will hurt you the most."

Chapter 17

"Fuck them muthafuckas," Rab said as he placed thirty bricks into his duffle bag. "I wish that motherfucker would have died in that bitch," he added, laughing it up with Batman.

"I wish I could've been there. I would have loved to see the look on his face right before he fell to his knees." Batman pictured Poppa Joe laid out holding his chest. "I know losing five million is a hard pill to swallow."

"Fuck him," Rab responded, meaning every word.

He wasn't even mad when Murder came to him claiming somebody hit the other spot for another hundred and fifty bricks. He didn't think twice about believing Murder took the opportunity to line his pockets. After all, he surely did.

"Give me a few days, I'll be right back at you," Rab said, throwing the duffel bag over his shoulder.

"Take your time. Ain't no rush," Batman assured him.

smiling know the reason for Poppa Joes heart attack was because of the robbery.

"Take my time? I'll fall back once I'm dead. Other than that, I got my foot on the gas. Ain't no cruise control with this shit. Like I said, I'll be back in a few days." Rab threw up the peace sign and pimped out the door.

Rab jumped in his SUV feeling himself. He was so caught

up in being the man and wanting Poppa Joe dead that he never paid attention to the move put into play that would ultimately uncover his betrayal.

*****

"Bitch, where you cop that chain from?" Freddie asked, pulling tight on Tamisha.

"Nigga, fall back," she said, looking down at the chain around her neck. "Nigga talking about he got eighty chains and ain't a motherfucker took one yet. Well, he can't say that shit no more," she added, exposing her hand.

Freddie wasn't going for what she was insinuating, though. "Bitch, stop playing."

"Believe what you want, but it is what it is," she said with a devious smile.

Freddie looked at her and could tell she wasn't faking.

"That's what the fuck I'm talking about! Bitch, you my soulmate." He playfully grabbed her up.

"What the fuck y'all got going on?" Tone asked as he walked into the room.

"Nigga, miss me with that jealousy. Mish done took ole boy up top. You see this shit?" Freddie told him and pointed to the chain.

"See what?" Tone yelled, recognizing whose chain it was. "You taking that shit back!"

He couldn't understand why she would do some dumb shit like that.

"Yeah right," Tamisha responded, looking at Tone like he was crazy. "You didn't take yours back, so what the fuck I look like taking mine back?" She tucked the chain back into her shirt.

Realizing who he was talking to, Tone just shook his

head. He took a deep breath trying to choose his words wisely. The last thing he wanted was for Tamisha to become argumentative and miss the logic of what he was saying.

"The difference between my situation and yours is when that nigga wakes up and realizes his chain is missing, who the fuck do you think is gonna be his number one suspect?" Tone said, unable to disguise his frustration.

Tamisha half listened, not really caring what he had to say. She felt like what's done was done; let the pieces fall wherever they may. If Cruzzi came playing and underestimated her gangsta, he would find his ass on the back of a milk carton.

"If you a real nigga, let's ride. No time for games or second-guessing," she rapped, letting him know where she stood regarding the situation.

"Talk that shit!" Freddie yelled, making matters worse. "Bitch, I'm riding," he told Tamisha and then looked over at Tone, who was shaking his head.

"You two stupid motherfuckers belong together." Realizing what he needed to do, Tone turned on his heels and walked away. "Let's see who laughs last," he said, thinking about the decision he made with the feds.

*****

Poppa Joe had been in the hospital a week and was scheduled to be released within the next few days. Despite still being stressed out, he was upbeat about getting out the hospital.

"I can't fucking wait to lay in my own bed, 'cause this shit here ain't what's happening," he joked with Sasha.

"I bet," she responded while rubbing his feet.

"Ooooh, bae, that shit feels good."

"Ain't this a Kodak moment?" Batman said, entering the

room carrying balloons and a stuffed bear.

"You got some nerve, white boy." Poppa Joe sat up in his bed, feeling some type of way.

"Calm down. I come in peace," Batman told him, pointing at the balloons and stuffed animal in his hands.

Poppa Joe tried to keep his cool and not expose his plans to kill his ass, but just looking at him, there was no denying what must be done.

"You rob me and then have the audacity to come visit me in the hospital like you fuck with me, you bitch-ass cracker?"

Poppa Joe attempted to get out bed and attack Batman, when a sharp pain shot straight through his heart. He collapsed on the floor grabbing his chest. The machines alerted the hospital staff that their patient was in distress.

Sasha jumped up. "Get out! Get the fuck out!"

Within seconds, doctors and nurses rushed in and ordered everyone to leave the room.

Smiling, Batman placed the stuffed bear and balloons on a nearby table and left. Never in his wildest dreams would he had ever imagined he would get the satisfaction of seeing Poppa Joe literally fall to his knees.

"I hope you die with yo' hands on your heart," he whispered while laughing to himself.

*****

"Did Sasha call you?" Stacks asked Murder as he entered the room.

"Yeah, she called me. I can't believe that fool showed up with balloons and shit. Had I been there—"

"We would've been bailing yo' ass out of jail," Angel said, interrupting their conversation. "I'm kinda glad you weren't," she continued as she took a seat next to her man. "The last thing we need on top of everything else already going on is you fighting an assault case against a police officer."

"True that," Stacks agreed, sitting across from them.

For the next few hours, the men discussed their next course of action while Angel fell back.

"Not that that's out the way, what's the situation with Rab's bitch ass?" Murder asked, although he already knew the answer to his own question.

"That nigga ain't missed a beat. It's like he doesn't give a fuck," Stacks replied, expressing how he felt. "I even sent one of my plays to cop a joint from him to see if the shit was ours or not."

"Was it?" Murder asked.

Stacks looked at him as if to say, *Nigga please*, before responding, "You better believe it."

*****

While Poppa Joe was laid up trying to recover, Sasha got with Tone to make sure he was still onboard to handle Batman's ass.

"Just handle it and I'll make sure we get paid," she said, trying to convince Tone to go ahead and body Batman.

"I hear you, but business is business. I want half up front and the rest when I put that motherfucker down," he told her, not trying to hear anything else. "Word on the streets is yo' boy got took up top by some muthafucka he wants killed," Tone pressed, wanting her to confirm or dismiss the rumor.

Sasha wasn't in the mood to even entertain the rumors. She wanted Batman dead as bad as Poppa Joe, and anyone who talked about anything outside of that objective might as well have been speaking a foreign language.

"I'm standing here trying to put money in our pockets and you're worried about a rumor?" She looked at Tone like he couldn't be serious. "Where's Freeze Pop? I know he ain't trained to go," she asked, hoping to throw him off like he wasn't about that life.

"Bitch, kill that noise. My nigga moves when I move, and we ain't moving until that weak-hearted nigga separates mine from his," he responded, letting her know what the business was.

"If that nigga falls out again, then what, Sasha? Huh?" He paused, looking for her to respond. "Because a dead man doesn't care who he owes."

Tone went on until she couldn't take any more.

"Okay, Tone, you made your point."

Unable to look him in the eyes, she turned away. Sasha was so consumed with wanting Batman dead that she almost lost sight of the ultimate goal, which was getting paid and leaving this life behind.

"I hope so, 'cause you on some other shit." He walked up behind her. "Get that money and I'll handle mine. Believe that," he told her, then kissed her on the neck. "I love you,."

He turned her around to look at him.

"I want this money so bad I can taste it. That money is our way out, to leave this life behind so I can share my life with the only female who has ever loved me for me and not..."

As he continued to pour his heart out, Sasha stood there in his arms almost on the verge of tears. She couldn't believe he was finally seeing all the things she'd been saying and envisioning from the start.

"I love you more!" She kissed her man passionately.

"Don't say another word. Make love to me," he told her.

Putting everything aside, she walked to the bedroom to be as one with her man.

Chapter 18

Rapping the lyrics to Meek Mills' "Tony Story, Part Two", Rab exited his SUV with a duffel bag loaded with fifty of those things he had just picked up from Batman. For the past few weeks, he'd been hunting the streets and adding a few extra points to his already-high ticket, making himself more money than he could ever make rocking with Poppa Joe.

Not long after he entered his spot, someone was at the door.

"Wait a minute!" he yelled, sliding the bag off his shoulder and setting it on the floor. "Girl, I thought I made it quite clear not to—"

He stopped mid-sentence when he saw it wasn't his girl at his door.

"Damn, nigga, the way you're looking, I take it I'm not who you were expecting," Murder said, inviting himself in.

"That you ain't, even if you were wearing a dress," Rab quickly responding, trying to act like everything was everything as he closed the door.

"You would definitely love that." Murder proceeded to walk into the living room as if the place belonged to him.

Rab cursed at himself for assuming he knew who was at the door and was even madder that he hadn't put away the duffle bag.

"So what brings you my way?" Rab asked, joining Murder in his living room.

"I just left Poppa Joe and wondered why you haven't come to see him?" he inquired, looking at Rab for some type of explanation.

"To be honest, I can't stand to see my guy laid up in the hospital like that," He replied, then motioned for Murder to follow him into the kitchen. "I'd rather wait until he comes home, you feel me?"

Rab glanced over his shoulder to make sure he was behind him.

"No doubt, fam," Murder said, faking like he understood.

Murder wasn't into small talk, and once they entered the kitchen, he ended it.

"I just want to know why, Rab? Why?"

"Why what?" Rab asked, not knowing his betrayal had been uncovered.

When he turned around, he was surprised to find himself staring down the barrel of a gun.

"Whoa, Murder! What the fuck?" Rab hoped like hell that Murder was trying to punk him.

"Seriously, nigga? How long did you think you could continue living a double life? How long?" Murder yelled, wanting to spark Rab's dumb ass up so bad that his hands began to sweat.

Rab stood there looking stupid as he tried to think of some type of response.

"Murder, I don't...I don't know what's going on or what the hell you're talking about. It's obvious you got me mixed up with someone else."

"Naw, pimpin', ain't no mix up at all. You sold out yo' Shamar and KC, the two guys who would've followed you until the end of the world. And in exchange for what, Rab?"

154

Murder shook his head as he looked at the man who he once considered to be family. "I hope it was worth it," he said before throwing a pair of handcuffs at Rab and knocking his ass out to total darkness.

Ten minutes later when Rab regained consciousness, he found himself tied up in a chair positioned in the middle of the kitchen.

"That's right. Come on back to life," Stacks said when he saw Rab move. "I know you think this shit is a dream." He drew back his arm and punched him in the face. "But it ain't."

Thinking about his betrayal and him sleeping with the enemy, Stacks went Mike Tyson on his ass, hitting him with all types of combinations.

"Hold on, Stacks," Murder said, stopping Stacks in the middle of his assault. "This nigga's been eating good. I found close to a mill in cash and fifty of those things in a duffle bag. I'd say we did alright."

Murder handed Stacks a towel to wipe the sweat off his face.

"Go load everything up while I have a few parting words with this turncoat-ass nigga," Murder told him, then looked back at Rab's swollen face.

"A'ight I'ma go do that," Stacks told him, but before leaving, he turned on his heels and suckerpunched Rab one last time. "Yeah, bitch! That was for Poppa Joe!"

Stacks felt better knowing it would be the last time he saw Rab breathing.

Murder waited until his man left out the kitchen before addressing Rab.

"It's crazy how you trust that blue-eyed nigga over the niggas who you played with in the sandbox. The same niggas who watched our mothers turn tricks to keep the lights on and keep food on the table. For a motherfucker who don't know nothing about the struggle, for a motherfucker that would rather lock yo' ass up than set you free. You're a stupid motherfucker."

Murder grabbed the container of gasoline beside him. Rab eyes grew big as Murder soaked him in the gasoline. He tried his best to plead his case and beg for his life through the duct tape over his mouth.

"Nigga, it's too late for explanations. Save that shit for a motherfucker who cares, 'cause it damn sure ain't me."

Murder struck a match and stared at Rab for a moment before throwing it at his feet.

"Columbus on fire, you bitch-ass nigga," he said, watching the flames engulf his body. "Say what's up to Lucifer for me."

He then turned and walked out the house without looking back and certainly without any remorse.

*****

"Ahhh! I can't believe this shit!" Batman screamed, knocking over the computer on his desk at the sub-station.

His crew stood back not knowing why he was acting out over a nigga they were going to kill anyway.

"Batman, it ain't that serious," one of the vice officer said, trying to calm him down.

"What the fuck did you just say?" Batman grabbed the young man by the collar. "I just lost fifty joints behind this shit."

Batman punched him in the mouth, taking his frustration out on him. Big Country and the rest of the crew rushed to pulled Batman off their fellow officer.

"Get your fucking hands off me!" he yelled out of breath, looking down at the young man who he had assaulted. "That will teach you to keep your mouth shut and stay out of my business."

Batman kicked him one last time before walking off and grabbing his keys. He needed to relieve some tension, and what better way to do that than to go fuck something. While heading home, he couldn't believe his luck. He had caught Murder in traffic. However, just when he was about to get on his ass, he noticed Murder was being followed.

"Oh shit!"

Batman turned off and headed in the opposite direction, wondering how long the feds had been on Murder like that. Batman busted a few corners and continued looking in his rearview mirror to make sure he wasn't being followed, but just like a bad nightmare, he peeped them on his ass, as well.

"Damn!" he said, wondering how long this had been going on.

*****

"The proof is in the pudding. These guys are dirty cops. They're basically thugs with a badge, and I'm going to nail their asses to the wall right next to Poppa Joe and the rest of these guys we're about to drop an indictment on," the head director of the FBI said. "We got a lot going on. It's going to take a lot of hardwork to ride the ship and clean the city up," he continued.

Angel and her partner left the meeting trading notes to make sure they were on the same page.

"You're one of the best I've ever worked with," her partner commented while looking at the reports she had submitted.

"Why wouldn't I be?" she responded, then smacked her partner on the ass. "I hope you can handle all ten inches," she added, reminding him of their bet.

"You got me fucked up."

His reply caused Angel to laugh.

"So what did we agree to then?" she asked, giving him a chance to rethink his previous proposition.

"It damn sure wasn't that," he responded, hoping she wasn't serious.

"Well, you better pay up on mine while you playing." Angel blew him a kiss as she pimped off.

*****

"Your girl is going to get her head knocked off," Poppa Joe told Sasha no sooner than she walked in the room.

"Boy, please! You've been in this hospital damn near three weeks, and here you are talking about my girl and you having issues. What we need to be doing is getting at Batman's ass," Sasha said, sticking with the business versus the bullshit about her girl.

"True that, but I just got off the phone with Gucci. He's at shorty's head, and being that's yo' girl, I wanted to pull your coat tail about it." Truthfully, Poppa Joe didn't care one way or the other because he had no love for the bitch.

Sasha paused for moment wondering what Tamisha could have possibly done to have Gucci at her neck. Then she remembered who she was dealing with.

"What did she do?" Sasha hoped like hell she hadn't given Gucci a STD.

"The lil' bitch took something that didn't belong to her and that shit's gonna cost her. I hope it was worth it," Poppa Joe stated, letting his girl know the seriousness of the situation.

"Damn," she responded, shaking her head.

Even though Sasha and Tamisha had their issues, she never wished anything bad to come to her.

"Let me call her and see what I can do before things get out of hand. I'm sure there's a good reason for why she did

158

it…that's if she even did it."

Sasha knew there were always three sides to a story: his, hers, and the truth. Only time would tell which story coincided with the truth.

"Do whatever you want. I ain't got nothing to do with it. Lord knows I got my share of problems." With that, Poppa Joe ended the conversation.

"What's good, fam?" Murder said, entering the room looking and sounding a whole lot happier than usual.

"I've seen better days, but what's up with you?" Poppa Joe inquired after seeing the look on Murder's face.

"Have you seen the news lately?" Murder asked as he gave Sasha a hug and dapped up his man.

Poppa Joe could sense something was up by Murder's body language, his conversation, and the smile on his face. Instead of answering Murder's question with a question, he changed the channel to catch Channel 10's six o'clock news. For the next ten minutes, Sasha sat quietly watching and incessantly praying that the news wouldn't report that Batman was dead. She could not stand the thought of her blood, sweat, and tears having been in vain during all of this, and even worst, missing out on her payday.

"What the fuck!" Poppa Joe yelled as the news reported the tragic killing of another one of his men. "I'm tired of playing with this motherfucker. I don't even care anymore. I'll kill them my goddamn self," he vented, attempting to get out of his bed.

Seeing the look on Poppa Joe's face, he made the situation right.

"Naw, fam, it ain't nothing like that. I was the one who sent that motherfucker to his maker."

His revelation took Poppa Joe and Sasha by surprise.

"You what?" Poppa Joe said in disbelief, hoping he wasn't hearing correctly.

"It's a long story," Murder told him.

"I don't give a fuck how long it is. Put me down with something." Poppa Joe waited for Murder to explain, because right about then, he wasn't feeling him.

Murder didn't hesitate to inform Poppa Joe about Rab's double life and how he uncovered his betrayal.

"So you're telling me the motherfucker laid down with that snake and plotted against me?"

Poppa Joe did not want to believe Rab would go against him like that.

"No doubt. That's why it was only right that I send him to the same place Batman sent Sherman and KC," Murder said, feeling good about how he handled the situation.

Sasha was stunned but happy that her payday was still out there to get. So, instead of commenting, she fell back and let them do them.

"If it's any consolation, I recovered fifty joints and over a mill in cash," Murder told Poppa Joe, knowing that in itself was something to smile about.

"You better believe that's good news," Poppa Joe replied as he calculated up in his head how far he was from that five million. "Even better news, I'm out of this bitch tomorrow," he added, thinking about all the moves he needed to make.

Chapter 19

When Batman peeped the feds on his bumper, he ordered his crew to fall back. He didn't know what had caused them to pick up on his scent and start following him, but from that point on, he would minimize what would be seen versus what they had already witnessed.

"Man, the hood's hotter than fish grease," Freddie commented, sharing his thoughts with his man.

"Why you say that? Them niggas out there acting a fool?" Tone asked, about to go out and bend a few corners.

"Hell naw. Them one motherfuckers circling the block like a motherfucker."

Tone stopped dead in his tracks. The mere mention of the feds caused his heart to skip a beat. He knew what was coming down the pipeline, and every day was like living on the run, not knowing which day would be your last.

"Are they acting like they're looking for somebody or are they just on some bullshit?" Tone asked, trying to get some feedback on how things were looking on the streets.

"Nigga, I didn't stay out there long enough to ask them." Freddie laughed at him for asking such a question. "But go on and take yo' ass out there, and when you see one of them, ask them."

Freddie laughed even more, feeling like he had just made the funniest comment in the world. Tone stood there not knowing if he should try his hand or fall back.

"Yeah right," Tone said, deciding to sit his ass down.

"That's the best decision you've made in a while," Freddie said as he sparked up a blunt.

Consumed with his thoughts, he never heard Freddie calling his name. The only way Freddie finally got his attention was when he threw a pillow at him.

"Damn, fam, you really been acting funny lately. It's like something's going on and you ain't telling me."

"What are you insinuating?" Tone retorted, not knowing how to take what his man was saying.

True enough, he was hiding something but revealing his hand wasn't an option.

"That's what the fuck I'm talking about. A nigga can't even talk to you without you getting all on the defensive. If there's something you need to get off your chest, don't bite your tongue on my account."

Freddie gave Tone the opportunity to do just that.

"Don't pay me any attention. I'm just focused on getting this money," Tone told him, speaking some real shit to cover his betrayal.

"I hope that's what it is, my nigga."

Freddie had a funny feeling but shrugged it off, believing the story Tone shot at him. He knew his man wasn't a stone-cold killer like himself. This murder shit was embedded deep within Freddie, unlike Tone who committed random acts of murder only when absolutely necessary. Freddie was a real-live killer who didn't hesitate when it came time to pull the trigger.

*****

Poppa Joe hadn't been home ten minutes before he started directing traffic. He needed to put together a few moves in order to make up for that five-million-dollar deficit. The fifty joints and one million dollars they retrieved from Rab was a good start.

"I'm telling you take the shake out and replace with acetyl, baking soda, or whatever the fuck you find. I don't give a fuck what it turns out to be. Press it, wrap it, and slang that shit out the door," Poppa Joe said, ending that call and answering his other phone.

"Talk to me," he told the caller and then listened as they spoke. "Naw, I'ma stay out of the limelight for a minute and let motherfuckers think a nigga is still laid up," he responded before ending that call, as well.

Poppa Joe looked up at his girl. "I need you to get at ole boy and them. Let them know it's on the floor."

He was tired of playing games with Batman. Sasha couldn't be happier.

"I got you, bae," she said, then bent down to give him a kiss before going to deliver his message.

"I already know." He smacked her on the ass as she walked away.

Just then, another one of his phones rang.

"Talk to me," he said, answering it.

Ready to put everything in motion, Sasha took off. She placed several calls to Tone, but he didn't answer.

"A'int that about a bitch!" she yelled as she hit the highway. "I'm trying to get this money and yo' punk ass is screening calls," she mumbled to herself, heading to her girl's spot until he decided to return her call.

Ten minutes later, she pulled up in front of her old residence.

"Damn, I'm gonna miss this place." She sat there for a minutes reliving all her memories from over the years, good and bad. "But not enough to stay," she said to herself, laughing as she made her way inside the building.

The moment Sasha let herself in, she found her girl coming out the bedroom.

"Hey, girl," Sasha greeted, closing the door behind her. "I was in the area and—"

She stopped mid-sentence when she saw a naked male exiting the bathroom.

"Oh, my bad. I didn't know you had company," Sasha apologized as the gentleman hurried into the bedroom. "Oooh, bitch, who was that?" she demanded to know while putting her purse on the endtable.

"Girl, please," Layla responded with a smile, heading toward the refrigerator. "That's my boo Chin."

Sasha sat there trying to get the juice on her girl's new boo thang, who eventually got dressed and then came back out to be introduced.

"I'ma let you know one thing, Mr. Chin. Hurt my girl if you want, but I'ma fuck you up if you do," Sasha playfully said, giving her girl the thumbs-up.

"That's the least of your worries," he responded, referring to something totally different than what she was thinking.

Chin gave Layla a kiss and told her to call him later. Then before making his exit, he turned toward Sasha and assured her that they would meet again. As soon as he left out the door, Sasha shared some news with her girl.

"Let me tell you what yo' girl done did now. The stupid bitch robbed Gucci for one of his chains."

"Get the fuck out of here! That's what that nigga gets. He should've chosen me," Layla responded, trying to make light of the situation. "But, seriously, I wish I could turn back time and shield her from everything versus exposing her to everything."

Layla felt greatly responsible for the way Tamisha had

164

turned out.

"Bitch, that ain't yo' burden to carry." Sasha hoped Layla agreed with her so she wouldn't continue to feel the way she felt. "She might be stupid," she added, knowing stupid people do crazy shit.

"That she is," Layla concurred.

Sasha's phone began to ring and she looked at the Caller ID before answering.

"So we're screening calls now?" she asked Tone, who was on the other end.

"Just save it. I'll be pulling down on you in a minute."

He ended their call without even saying goodbye.

"Who was that?" Layla questioned as Sasha stood up to leave.

"Our ticket out of this life we've grown accustomed to living."

Without another word, she blew her girl a kiss and pimp-walked out the door.

Chapter 20

With the money now in place, Tone was ready to put everything in motion. They had gone over the plan many times and knew their roles and positions well.

"Bitch, where the fuck you at?" Tone yelled into the phone. "If you ain't here in ten minutes, don't even worry about coming because we won't be here."

He hung up without waiting on her response.

Tamisha looked at her phone, not believing how Tone was acting. She had just left out east throwing a few back at the 57 Nightclub and was no more than a few minutes from pulling down on them.

As she headed down Livingston while listening to some classic Biggie, someone ran into the back of her as she sat at a red light.

"What the fuck!" she screamed, almost catching whiplash.

She looked in the rearview mirror to see a tinted-out SUV.

"Oh, this motherfucker's gonna pay!" she yelled, jumping out her Lexus.

It was a little past one o'clock in the morning as she stood near the driver's side window shouting for the person to get out of the vehicle.

"You got me fucked up! Roll down this motherfucking window! I'ma beat that ass!"

She just knew it had to be a non-driving female behind the wheel.

"That's right, bitch! Rolls that motherfucker down!"

Tamisha made the mistake of standing too close to the vehicle, because in one motion, a hand reached out and snatched her head into the window.

"Bitch, you thought this shit was a game?" the driver said, placing his glock to the side of her head.

Tamisha smiled. She recognized the voice as death loomed in the air like an elephant in the room. She could feel death coming but didn't fear it like others who got caught slipping. Instead of begging and pleading for her life, she embraced her fate.

"Naw, bitch-ass nigga, you thought it was a game having eighty chains and thinking a bitch wasn't gonna take one," she retorted, not giving him the satisfaction of her bitching up.

"Say no more," he said, blasting shorty's wig back as the song that instigated it all played in the background.

Go dig yo' partner up; bet he can't say shit; and looking for the kid, I'll be in zone six.

He pulled off not worrying about a thing.

*****

"Man, if this bitch ain't here within the next ten minutes, then fuck her," Tone said.

While pacing back and forth, he attempted to call her one last time. They had already been waiting an hour from the time Tone previously called and she claimed she was on her way.

168

"Let's ride," Freddie told him, not willing to wait another minute. "We can handle this shit ourselves," he added as he gathered Czod and Jesus before heading out the door.

For the next twenty minutes, each man rode in silence knowing that after tonight things would never be the same. It was a little past three o'clock in the morning when they finally pulled into Batman's complex. Like a thief in the night, they exited the car and gained access into Batman's condo. Once inside, they stood over him and his baby mama. Both were sound asleep and unaware of the two people who came to claim their lives.

"Ain't this cute," Freddie said, turning on the overhead lights in the room.

Tasha B was the first to wake up.

"Oh my God!" she screamed upon seeing the two masked men pointing their guns at them.

Her cry instantly caused Batman to jump up out of his slumber.

"Whoa!" He couldn't believe what he had waken up to. "Look, I don't know what type of drugs y'all are on, but I'm a police officer and I know y'all don't want—"

"Don't want what, Batman?" Freddie said, cutting him off and removing his ski mask.

Once Tasha B saw his face, she was slightly shocked, but then again, who would be crazy enough to fuck with Batman besides Freeze Pop? Then she glanced at the other male standing on the opposite side of the room and knew it couldn't be anyone else but her cousin.

"Tone, I know that's you over there," she said, causing Batman to look at her sideways.

"You know these guys?" he questioned Tasha B, wondering what the hell was going on.

"Does she?" Tone finally responded, taking off his mask, as well.

Batman stared at Tone, whose face looked familiar. Suddenly it hit him.

"You're the one from the dice game who got away when shots were fired." Batman recalled the incident as if it just happened yesterday.

"And you're the one who rubbed another fuck the wrong way," Tone shot back, letting it be known they weren't there by accident.

The hairs on Batman's neck instantly stood up. Out of all the enemies he had, he knew there was only one who had enough balls to shoot a play like this at him. One person that would bring the fight to his doorstep versus leaving it in the streets because shit had gotten too personal.

"Poppa Hoe finally grew a set, huh?" Batman said, throwing his suspicion out there.

"I wouldn't know. He definitely put that money in place, though." Tone pointed his gun at Batman's head.

Batman threw his arms up like they would stop the bullets. "Hold on. If it's money you want, I'll pay you double to walk away," he offered, hoping to play on their greed.

"That shit sounds good, Batman, but you ain't working with those type of numbers," Tone replied, ready to knock his wig back.

"You'd be surprised, young man." Batman pointed to a duffle bag in the corner.

When Freddie looked inside the bag, he couldn't believe the contents inside.

"Whoa, Batman! Where the fuck did you get these type of ends from?" Freddie showed Tone the money inside the bag.

"That's beside the point," Batman said, hoping the money would distract the two men enough for him to make his move.

As if in slow motion, he went for his pistol resting underneath the pillow. Before he could pull it out, Freddie let Czod and Jesus spark, catching Batman multiple times in the

170

chest and mid-section. Batman still managed to get off one shot. However, it was one shot he instantly wished he had never shot, because he ended up hitting the person he never intended on harming.

"Ahhh!" Tasha B screamed, grabbing her stomach.

The look in Batman's eyes right before he took his last breath was one of regret. He died wishing he had never tried such a stupid move. Maybe then his chocolate young thing and unborn child could see another day.

With all the noise from the shots fired and Tasha B's screaming, Freddie knew half the occupants of the complex had called 911. Without thinking, he grabbed Tasha B by the head and put two shots in her to silence her.

"Nigga, snap out of it!" he yelled at Tone. "Grab the money and let's bounce."

Freddie pushed Tone to move, but before leaving, he checked to make sure Batman was dead. Upon exiting the building, they saw every neighbor was outside with their phones.

"Oh shit!" Freddie yelled, realizing it was all or nothing. *Take no prisoners.*

He let Czod and Jesus reach out and touch anybody in sight. Tone followed up but had been smart enough to put his ski mask back on before he exited Batman's condo. As they rushed towards their getaway car, Tone looked back to see all the bodies that he and Freddie had put down.

"Get the fuck in the car!" Freddie yelled, firing at any and everything after reloading both of his guns.

They both jump in and sped off into the night with their hearts beating like a drum. Five minutes into their ride, Tone was the first to speak.

"Everything that could go wrong did." Tone looked over at his man and waited for him to respond.

"Just shut the fuck up and drive," Freddie replied,

thinking of the worst-case scenario. Regardless of how he tried to dress it up in his mind, he knew shit was bad. "Too many people, too many people...and I know I didn't kill them all," he expressed, fearing someone had seen his face.

"You good, fam. We dropped a lot of motherfuckers, and the motherfuckers we didn't get probably won't remember because of the flying bullets. Plus, it was dark as hell."

He was telling his man what he wanted to hear while figuring out how to get far away from his ass.

"I don't know, Tone. That shit sounds good, but..." Freddie stared out the window hoping his man was right.

Tone glanced over at him. He knew he couldn't allow himself to be caught up in no cop-killing shit. Freddie was his brother from another mother and he truly loved him, but Tone loved himself and his freedom more.

"I'm sorry, fam."

"Sorry for—"

Before Freddie could finish his sentence, Tone blasted his man, splattering his brains all over the passanger side window. A tear escaped his eyes for the act of ultimate betrayal he had just committed. Reaching over Freddie's dead body, he opened the door and pushed him onto the freeway, then took the next exit. There was only one way to make the situation right.

*****

The news of a rampage shooting that left several dead and many wounded, along with a police officer and his pregnant girlfriend who were slayed within their home, overshadowed the news of Tamisha and Freddie's deaths. Once the news reached the head director of the FBI, he wasted no time putting in the order to bring everybody in from Poppa Joe, the Short North posses, and the dirty cops. The FBI, U.S.

Marshals, ATF, and Columbus PD went throughout the city conducting raids. One by one, they were marched in and booked into Franklin County Jail. All were unaware of the seriousness of the charges.

"What the fuck y'all got me charged with?" one person yelled while watching as a few more of his guys were being booked.

"Don't worry, your lawyer will be here with your federal complaint."

Wondering what kind of federal case he could possibly have, the dude quickly shut up, not saying another word.

Then the moment of truth came when about thirty Brittany Hills niggas came through the door along with Poppa Joe.

"We'll be out of here within an hour," he told his crew when Big Country and four of his fellow officers were brought in handcuffed.

Seeing that caused waves of shock to travel throughout the holding cells. Many finally came to the realization that some serious shit was going down.

"What the fuck?" Poppa Joe thought it was some type of joke. That is until they placed Big County in a holding cell across from them. "This shit just got real," Poppa Joe finished saying, turning to look at his man.

Before he could say anything, one of his guys asked, "Do y'all think this has something to do with Batman getting murdered?"

All eyes were drawn to him.

"Where you getting this information from?" Poppa Joe asked.

He wanted to know, because if it was the truth, then they were only down there for questioning and would be set free later that day. The thought brought a smile to his face.

While Poppa Joe questioned his man in an attempt to get

more details, Murder quietly stood there waiting to make his one call. He didn't know what was going on or why Poppa Joe entertained the conversation about Batman's murder. True enough, it might have been part of the reason they were down there, but his gut feeling was telling him there was more to it than just that. Right then, the only thing he wanted to do was call his baby and give her instructions. However, his thoughts were interrupted when Stacks slapped him on the shoulder and pointed in the direction of the mayhem.

"Oh hell naw!" Murder and Poppa Joe both yelled while staring at Angel bringing two guys into booking.

Angel was dressed in riot gear with a FBI badge hanging from her neck. If things weren't serious before, better believe they were now.

"She's the police," Poppa Joe whispered as he slid down the wall with both hands covering his face.

Murder, on the other hand, could not contain his disbelief. "Angel, you ain't no police! You ain't no police," he yelled out as he hung onto the window.

The whole scene was reminiscent of the movie *In Too Deep* starring LL Cool J. When you realize the one person you trusted the most could be the same one to betray you.

*****

By mid-afternoon, the news was buzzing with reports about the murder of Batman and his pregnant girlfriend, the arrests that had been made, and a video of two suspects gunning down eyewitnesses as they made their escape from a murder scene.

"Sasha, did you see Freddie on the news? I know you know who the other person is in the video," Layla said, causing Sasha to hang up on her hot ass.

"This bitch got the nerve to be talking like that over my

phone," Sasha said to herself.

Each time Layla tried to call back, Sasha sent her to voicemail.

True enough, she knew it was Tone on that video, but she hoped he didn't get caught out there like Freddie, who had exposed his face.

"Damn, Tone, what went wrong?" Sasha mumbled as she continued watching the police destroy Poppa Joe's house during the raid.

She was just waiting for them to finish so that she could lock up and get in the wind. As she waited, she played out all the different scenarios she could imagine…this not being one of them.

*****

"Boy, have you lost yo' goddamn mind?" Ms. Jones yelled at her son. She didn't want to believe what she had seen on the news. "I'ma tell you something because you're my son and I love you unconditionally. Life is about self-preservation, and if you put the next motherfucker before your own, you ain't no son of mine."

In other words, she was telling him indirectly that dead men don't talk or point fingers.

"Don't even worry about that, Mom. Just keep watching the news and know you ain't raise no dummy."

Tone said goodbye before ending the call. Then he fell back into his chair and continued watching the news as all of his guys were arrested, except Tommy C, Chin, and himself. It wasn't a secret that they were definitely looking for him. Not for the murder of Batman, but for the murders he committed with his Short North niggas.

"I'm glad I prepared for this moment," he said to himself, feeling comfortable ducked off in his spot that no one knew about.

Tone looked at the duffle bag filled with money and thought, *Damn! That motherfucker got arrested before I could collect the rest of my money, but fuck it. Batman covered the other half and then some.*

Laughing, he was ready to execute his plan to leave the country.

*****

The next day, the city was glued to their flat-screen TVs awaiting the six o'clock news. Tamisha's murder was mentioned, but it wasn't the breaking news. Freddie Jackson aka Michael Jackson, aka Freeze Pop, aka Mr. Freeze had been found dead on the side of the highway. He had been the number one suspect in the complex shooting where a cop was killed. The people on the streets and those who were locked up had their own opinion of what they would have done if they were in Tone's shoes.

With niggas running their mouths like a bad case of diarrhea, along with Crime Stoppers putting a bag on top of a nigga's head for any information, Tone couldn't win. It was only a matter of time before it reached the head director of the FBI.

"It's been brought to my attention that we might have the identity of the second shooter who tried his best to distance himself by killing his partner in crime. It's also my understanding this same young man is already a fugitive at large inducted on the Short North indictment. C'mon, ladies and gentlemen, let's pull together all our resources and bring this guy in immediately."

The head director distributed an enlarged picture of their suspect to the law enforcement before ending the briefing.

"Oh my God," Angel said, not believing her eyes.

"What is it?" her partner quickly asked when he saw the look on her face.

"I know something a lot of people would love to know," she whispered to him while leaving the briefing.

"Talk to me, partner," he whispered back as he followed behind her, hoping like hell they could pull off the unthinkable and bring in Mr. Jones before anyone else.

"I know what he loves and who he loves. I definitely know where he's going, 'cause one thing for certain and two things for sure, the power of the pussy is phenomenal."

She laughed as she strutted off.

Chapter 21

"That fuck nigga killed my girl and I'm gonna have his ass," Layla told Sasha as they packed their things.

"I don't believe so, Layla. Shit just doesn't add up. Plus–"

"Plus nothing!" she yelled, throwing down everything she had been holding. "You so blinded by love that you're gonna let this motherfucker get away with killing yo' girl? He already showed what he was capable of, and you're still gonna stand there and defend him? Bitch, are you that dick drunk?" Layla spat, ready to beat some sense into her girl.

After going back and forth, Sasha realized she didn't know for sure if he had done it or not. Regardless of that, he held the bag to their future. So to save face and remain loyal to her girls, she agreed to allow the triple cross to be put into play since the cross and double cross had already been put down.

"Don't even trip. We're gonna get up with this nigga, leave the country, and live the life we dreamed of living," Layla assured Sasha. "Now let's finish packing and get the fuck out of here."

*****

For the last four hours, Angel and her partner had been sitting outside of Sasha's old apartment building waiting on her to make a move. She knew within her heart that Sasha would lead them to Tone or Tone would find his way to her. Either way, they knew Sasha was the key.

"You really think he's going to fuck with his ex knowing the type of heat on his ass?" her partner asked, keeping his attention on all activity coming up and down the street.

"I'll bet my last dollar on it," she replied.

No sooner had she spoken those words, Sasha and her friend exited the building with bags in hand.

"Here we go!" Angel started the car as she watched Layla and Sasha throw their luggage in the trunk of the rental car.

"Jump in. I'll drive," Layla told Sasha, getting comfortable before pulling off.

Ten minutes into the ride as they were speeding down I-270, Layla started receiving texts, which prompted her to start asking questions concerning Tone.

"We're supposed to meet ole boy at—"

"Just drive. I'm texting him back now." Sasha still felt uneasy about crossing the love of her life.

After getting the directions where to meet him, tears began running down Sasha's face as she wondered if it was all worth the pain, the loss, and the heartache of betraying the one she loved more than life itself.

"When does it all end?" Sasha said, directing the question to her girl as the weight of the situation came crashing down on her all at once.

Layla looked at Sasha as if to say, *Bitch, straighten up!*

"It all will end once that nigga is six feet under pushing up daisies and not a moment sooner," Layla replied, not showing any empathy for the tears her girl was shedding. "You're crying over that bitch-ass nigga that hasn't shed one tear for our girl. Are you serious, Sasha? Is it worth turning a

180

blind eye? Is it fucking worth—" Layla continued, painting a picture.

She painted a picture of a person who would stare you in the eyes and, while holding that same stare, kill you without thinking twice about it. Sasha listened to everything she said and wasn't moved by any of it. She was in love with someone who she wasn't ready to let go of or depart from.

"Okay, Layla! It's not my fault that I'm in love with the man who possibly killed one of my best friends. I can't help who I fell in love with," she yelled, wishing she didn't have to choose.

*****

With an all-out manhunt going on, Tone made his escape to Cincinnati, Ohio. He sat comfortably on a small airstrip on the edge of town sipping on some Dom P.

"Mama, I made it!" he joked with himself while awaiting his baby's arrival.

He was in possession of close to over a million dollars in cash, rocking Herdo's BHP chain in plain sight, and not worried about a thing.

"Sir Jones," the pilot said, interrupting his vibe. "The jet will be refueled and ready for takeoff within the next fifteen minutes," he told him, then motioned for the stewardess to walk with him back to the cockpit.

As Tone sat on the jet ready to take off and with thoughts of never returning to the states again, he received a text from Sasha letting him know she was close and couldn't wait to be in his arms. Tone smiled as he texted back, assuring her that the life they once lived, they would never have to live again.

*****

"Do you think we should call for backup?" Special Agent Johnson asked his partner, feeling they were close to apprehending their suspect.

"Don't get scared now. It's only one of him and two of us. How's he going to win?" Angel said, glancing at her partner as they turned onto a gravel road.

Closing in on their suspect, their adrenaline started pumping. Their hands began to sweat and their hearts beated faster.

"Where do you think this road leads to?" Special Agent Johnson asked, but his question was answered when the airstrip came into view in the distance. "C'mon, Angel. Speed up!" he ordered, seeing Sasha and her friend boarding a small jet.

Angel gunned the engine, kicking up gravel everywhere until they reached a security booth.

"FBI!" they yelled in unison, flashing their badges and hoping to gain entry.

"I don't care who you are. This is private property, and if you don't have clearance or a warrant, whatever business you have will have to be done on that side of the fence," the security officer stated, then pointed to behind them.

Angel and her partner looked on cursing as the jet taxied down the runway and took off into the air.

"Don't worry. The hunt had just begun."

Pulling out her phone, Angel placed a call to the Head Director of the FBI.

*****

Tone felt some type of way about Sasha bringing along her hating-ass girl.

"I thought you wanted to leave that life behind you?" Tone yelled once they were alone. "But you're gonna bring

182

that bitch along. I can't believe you, Sasha," he vented, shaking his head.

"I do and I have. That's why I'm not in Columbus mourning my girl's murder."

She brought up the subject of Tamisha to see what type of response she would get from him.

"It's crazy, Sasha. With everything going on, not once have I considered what you're going through. I'm sorry about your girl." He meant every word as he hugged his girl.

Her tears started to get the best of her as she reflected back on the past year and everything that had transpired.

"Tone..." She broke away from his embrace. "I need to know something, but before I ask you, I want you to know that I love you no matter what and there's nothing you can do or say that will change that."

Sasha paused to make sure he understood how sincere she was being.

"Did you kill Freddie?"

She used that question as the lead in to what she really wanted to know.

Tone's whole facial expression changed as he turned and walked away. Her question rocked him to his core. He honestly felt he had done what was best for them.

"Sasha, I can't stand here and lie to you, let alone try to justify my actions. It was either him or us, and I chose us," he confessed.

"Okay, bae, I understand. Now, my next question is just as important."

She walked up to him and took his hands in hers.

"Did you kill my girl?" she asked while staring into his eyes, searching them for any signs of deception.

"Hell no! I didn't have a reason to. Bae, I've never boxed anybody without good reason. Tamisha was family and never threw shade my way."

He hoped she believed him because it was the truth.

"Say no more. Just make love to me."

Sasha truly believed him and planned on telling him about Layla.

In the next room, Layla was texting with her boo and pledging her love and loyalty to him.

Us against the world, was the last thing she texted before calling it a night.

Chapter 22

Morning came too soon, and the non-stop ringing of Sasha's phone was their alarm clock.

"Will you please do something with that damn phone?" Tone yelled as he rolled over, ready to throw it out the window.

Looking at the Caller ID, Sasha knew it was Poppa Joe calling from the county jail. She felt bad for him and his situation, but she wouldn't dare answer his call while she was around Tone. He wouldn't understand, so to avoid stirring anything up, she simply turned off her phone.

"Shit, we might as well get up, get dressed, and go take a stroll along the coast," Tone said, turning over to give his baby a morning kiss.

"Oooh wee! Please go handle that." Sasha laughed and fanned her hand in front of her face as she slid out of the bed.

*****

Things couldn't be any better as they fed each another while looking off into the ocean.

"This is what I'm talking about. I can wake up to every day until the end of time as long as I'm with you," Tone proclaimed, taking in her beauty.

The rising sun created a beautiful orange glow on the clouds. The temperature was just right and the wind blew gently, making Sasha's nipples poke against the fabric of her shirt. She smiled as Tone licked his lips.

"I love when you do that."

"Do what?" he asked, even though he knew exactly what she was referring to.

Before Sasha could reply, Layla appeared out of nowhere, interrupting their moment.

"Ain't this cute?" she cooed, grabbing a piece of bacon off Sasha's plate and taking a bite. "I wish I had a camera 'cause this is definitely a Kodak moment."

Tone just looked at Sasha and shook his head as he stood up to leave.

"I'ma go take a swim while you and yo' girl spend some time together, 'cause there is definitely a crowd."

"And yo' bitch ass is the third wheel?" Layla said after Tone was far enough away not to hear her.

"I hope you're enjoying these last few moments with his ass 'cause I'm ready."

"No, Layla, he didn't do it. He didn't kill her. I can almost guarantee that," Sasha said, hoping to convince her.

Layla wasn't going for that, and she felt some type of way that her girl was entertaining the notion. "Tone's bitch ass didn't do it? You let this nigga stick his dick in you and whisper sweet nothings in your ear, and now you're on his side? Bitch, wake up!"

Frustrated, she threw a glass of water in Sasha's face.

"If that didn't wake yo' silly ass up, what will?" Layla stormed off, leaving Sasha alone to make her choice.

*****

Later that evening while Sasha was taking a swim in the

ocean, Tone relaxed on the sand sipping on a Long Island Iced Tea. Earlier in the day, Sasha had turned her phone back on to check her messages, but forgot to power it back off. When Sasha's phone rang, he started to answer it, but decided against it. However, whoever it was kept calling back to back.

Who the fuck is this? Tone said to himself as he picked up the phone and looked at the screen.

Recognizing the county number, he pressed five and waited for the caller to identify themselves.

"Sasha," the caller eagerly said.

"Naw, nigga, this ain't no damn Sasha," Tone finally responded, recognizing the voice on the other end.

"If it's not a problem, can I speak to her?" the caller asked as he tried to mask his disappointment that some guy was answering her phone.

Tone began to laugh, making Poppa Joe feel uncomfortable.

"Poppa Joe, you had yo' run with my bitch. Now find comfort in another man's arms," he shot, letting him have it.

Needless to say, Poppa Joe was surprised that the person on the phone knew who he was and about his situation.

"Miss me with all the bullshit and tell my bitch, yo' bitch, or *our* bitch that I'm on the phone," Poppa Joe demanded, getting mad that he found himself tongue wrestling with some nigga.

"That's one thing you'll never have to worry—"

Before Tone could finish his sentence, someone cut into the conversation.

"Damn, fam, you're a long way from home," the man said.

Tone damn near shit himself at the sight of him.

"Chin, what are you—"

Those were his last words before Chin put two in his dome.

Swimming to the shore, Sasha saw everything play out. It's like it all happened in slow motion. She rushed out the water screaming. She couldn't believe Layla's boyfriend had just killed the love of her life.

"No, Chin! No, Layla! He didn't do it," she yelled, running to her man. "Why, y'all? Why?" she cried, while cuddling Tone in her arms and rocking him back and forth. "I'm sorry, bae. I shoulda told you. I shoulda told you."

Chin knew he couldn't leave any witnesses behind. So, he put two in Sasha, as well.

"What the fuck!" Layla yelled, in shock that Chin had just killed Sasha. "This wasn't part of the plan!" She rushed to her girl's side.

"I know, and this ain't either," Chin said, putting three into her: two in her dome and one in her heart.

"Fam, what you kill the bitch for?" Tommy C asked as he appeared on the scene.

"Trust no bitch; love no hoe," Chin responded, looking at his man like he should've known that. "Did you find that nigga's money?" he asked while checking to make sure everybody was dead.

"You best believe I did." Tommy C held up the duffle bag.

With their work done, they turned and pimped off.

Poppa Joe stood holding the phone. He couldn't believe the events that transpired and how things unfolded. He wiped away the tear that fell for his baby Sasha. He had truly fallen in love with her and loved the way she blessed him, even in death.

"I'm closer to going home than I thought."

With a smile, he turned on his heels and yelled for the guard.

About the Author

Quintessa Turner is an up and coming novelist who shares her message by presenting characters who face real-life struggles and overcome them.

Before launching her literary career, Quintessa spent her younger years reading, developing business, and obtaining degrees. Many of the books she read she could relate to. The characters seemed so real that she could place herself in the lives of those she read about. She began to write poetry, but that dream died. After marrying and having children, the events that occurred around her inspired her to write urban fiction novels.

When not writing, Quintessa spends time with her family, runs a home care business with her business partner, and just enjoys life.

With the blessing of God, she will continue to be an inspiration to her readers and give them nothing but page-turners.

Other Books By Quintessa Turner

Available Now

Coming Soon